"Are you trying to seduce me?" Michael asked roughly.

"Yes," Raine said, surprised at herself. She'd never made advances to a man before, not like this. She wanted him to forget what he'd just seen in the garden, but she also wanted him to make love to her. "Can I seduce you?"

He pulled her harder against him. She was trying to distract him, and she was succeeding beautifully. Dark anger vied with bright desire. "You can try," he muttered, and skimmed his lips down her throat.

She threw her head back and arched her neck. There was tantalizing enjoyment in flirting with him, she discovered. This teasing prelude to lovemaking was like dancing through flames. Only there was no pain, just sweet heat. "How hard would I have to try?" she whispered.

"Not very hard at all. That's the hell of it." He brought his mouth to hers and nipped her lower lip with barely concealed violence.

An intense, aching hunger was building in the pit of her stomach. For six long years she'd repressed all feelings of the heart and body. Now passion and love burst free.

He tore his mouth from hers. "You're mine," he said.

"Yes."

He heard the helplessness in her answer but couldn't stop touching her everywhere. "You feel like heaven in my hands," he said fiercely. "What will you taste like . . . ?"

WHAT ARE *LOVESWEPT* ROMANCES?

They are stories of true romance and touching emotion. We believe those two very important ingredients are constants in our highly sensual and very believable stories in the *LOVESWEPT* line. Our goal is to give you, the reader, stories of consistently high quality that may sometimes make you laugh, sometimes make you cry, but are always fresh and creative and contain many delightful surprises within their pages.

Most romance fans read an enormous number of books. Those they truly love, they keep. Others may be traded with friends and soon forgotten. We hope that each *LOVESWEPT* romance will be a treasure—a "keeper." We will always try to publish

LOVE STORIES YOU'LL NEVER FORGET
BY AUTHORS YOU'LL ALWAYS REMEMBER

The Editors

LOVESWEPT® • 318

Fayrene Preston
The Pearls of Sharah II: Raine's Story

BANTAM BOOKS
TORONTO • NEW YORK • LONDON • SYDNEY • AUCKLAND

THE PEARLS OF SHARAH II:
RAINE'S STORY

A Bantam Book / April 1989

LOVESWEPT® and the wave device are registered
trademarks of Bantam Books, a division of
Bantam Doubleday Dell Publishing Group, Inc.
Registered in U.S. Patent
and Trademark Office and elsewhere.

If you would be interested in receiving protective vinyl
covers for your Loveswept books, please write to this address
for information:

Loveswept
Bantam Books
P.O. Box 985
Hicksville, NY 11802

ISBN 0-553-21969-3

Published simultaneously in the United States and Canada

Bantam Books are published by Bantam Books, a division
of Bantam Doubleday Dell Publishing Group, Inc. Its trademark, consisting of the words "Bantam Books" and the
portrayal of a rooster, is Registered in U.S. Patent and
Trademark Office and in other countries. Marca Registrada.
Bantam Books, 666 Fifth Avenue, New York, New York 10103.

PRINTED IN THE UNITED STATES OF AMERICA

O   0 9 8 7 6 5 4 3 2 1

The Pearls of Sharah series
is dedicated with all my love
to my sons,

Greg and Jeff,

two very special people.

Prologue

Far beneath the surface of the swelling waves, in
the dark, mysterious, primordial depths of the
sea, the pearls grew and waited.

Until . . .

King Darius was coming.

Princess Sharah sat by a pool of still water while
a handmaiden ran a comb through the shimmering length of her black hair. Lotus blossoms floated
on the pool that reflected the princess's serenely
beautiful face. But just as the deep water hid the
dark roots of the blossoms, so, too, did her serene
countenance hide troubled thoughts.

With a wave of her hand she dismissed the handmaiden. None of the servants had yet sensed their lord's approach, but Sharah did not need to see him or even to hear the soft tread of his footsteps to know he was near. She did not require Darius's presence to feel his every breath. She could not explain why this was, nor did she need to. She was a princess of the Karzana, a nomadic tribe, and she accepted that there were powers which could not be understood.

All she needed to know was that her blood sang when he strode through the halls of the great palace toward her private rooms here in the tower, and that the very air around her seemed to fill with excitement.

There was a stirring among her handmaidens. One of them tittered, then another. Ah, now they also knew he was coming.

Darius was drawing close.

On those nights when Darius came to her bedchamber, she accepted his attentions because circumstances had forced her to do so. She also writhed in pleasure beneath him, because he was a lover of great accomplishment. And afterward she held him through the night until dawn, because, secreted within her heart, was a profound and deep love for him.

But she was also proud, and she refused to surrender her soul to him as he was determined she would. . . .

With the power of a great wind Darius strode into the chamber and clapped his hands. "Leave us."

The serving girls bowed and dispersed.

Sharah lifted her head and gazed at him. Every line of his strong body bespoke command and power. Even without the royal robes he wore he would have looked kingly. Nevertheless, his *candy* was of bluish-purple; his sash was of cloth of gold; and his shawl was ornamented with rubies, emeralds, sapphires, and diamonds.

The gods had bestowed all the manly graces on Darius, Sharah thought once again, and she knew that hearts beat fast within the breasts of all the fair young women upon whom he deigned to look.

But it was only she he wanted. And so she waited.

He held out his hand to her. "Come here, my love."

The dark blue silk of her full trousers and tunic murmured as she rose and moved with unconscious grace toward him. "My lord?"

He cupped his fingers around her chin and lifted her face to his. "Five years, Sharah. Why do you still insist upon calling me 'my lord' when we're alone? I've asked you not to."

She cast her eyes downward. "You are King Darius, ruler of all Persia. I am your concubine."

He stifled his impatience. "You are my beloved."

"I am your property, taken from my people as you swept through my country in your quest to expand your empire."

"How could I have left you?" he whispered roughly. "One look at that beautiful face of yours and my heart was lost."

Her dark eyes flashed fire at him. "Yet you keep me prisoner."

"Prisoner, Sharah? Gaze around you. What do you see? This is not a prison. This is one of the finest rooms in the palace." In anger and frustration he jerked the miter from his head and hurled it across the room. "No, I am *your* prisoner."

Darius's temper was legendary, and his action would be guaranteed to send brave men scurrying for cover.

Sharah simply met his hard gaze with a soft question. "Then I'm free to leave?"

"You know I cannot allow that. I cannot live without you. I will not."

She smiled sadly and turned away.

He caught her by the shoulders before she could put distance between them and brought her back against his body. "Is my presence in your bed so displeasing to you?" he murmured, his mouth at her ear.

She closed her eyes as pleasure shivered through her. "You know it is not. You are a very skilled lover. My body responds to you even when my mind wills differently. But the blood of the Karzana that runs in my veins demands I must be free to go to my people when they need me."

"*I* need you. Give me your love, Sharah."

"Gladly. When you give me my freedom."

He sighed heavily and gradually his hands loosened on her shoulders until they dropped to his side.

The heat between their bodies disturbed her. She took several steps away before she faced him again.

He pulled a red bag from the folds of his *candy*. "I have brought you a present that I have had made especially for you." She did not respond. Darius smiled inwardly. His Sharah—so stubborn, so proud. "Hold out your hands," he said softly, and when she did, he pulled the silken strings loose and upended the contents into her hand. Out spilled a long rope of large, matched pearls. The clasp was a pearl that had grown in the shape of a heart.

Unable to stop the gasp of admiration that rose naturally to her lips, she lifted the necklace to the light. Each pearl was an object of perfect loveliness, creamy white in color, blushed with a soft pink.

Darius took them from her hands and carefully laid them around her neck. "These are my gift of love to you, Sharah," he said quietly.

She looked down at the pearls that fell over her breasts to reach to her knees, and within her proud soul another scar was carved. Darius had given her the extraordinary pearls to try to make her forget that even birds could fly free, but not she.

She raised her head, sending her hair rippling to her waist, a silken black cascade. "Am I free to do as I wish with these pearls?"

"Of course. They are yours."

She moved to one of the tall, arched tower windows. "Then I may throw them away?"

An expression of surprise crossed his face, but he nodded, wanting to humor her out of her sad mood. "Yes, although I wish you would not. It took a great deal of time and effort to collect pearls so perfectly matched."

"But may I throw them away?" she insisted.

Frowning, he said, "If you so desire."

She glanced out the window to the ground some hundreds of feet below. "And may I jump after them?"

"No!" Horrified, he raced across the room to pull her away from the window. "Sharah, what are you thinking of? If you jumped, you would be killed."

Gravely she stared up at him. "So I am free to do with the pearls what I will, but not myself."

"Sharah—"

"You gave me the pearls freely as a gift of your love. I, too, want to give you my love freely. But as long as I am kept against my will, I cannot."

"Sharah, how can I let you go?" His voice broke with his anguish. "You are my life."

She touched his face, so dear to her heart, and softly smiled. "No, Persia is your life. But you will have me, my dearest. Let me live as I was meant to be—free, like all those of my tribe, to shelter under the wide sky and ride with the winds. If you do this for me, I promise I will always come back to you."

"Sharah, I cannot . . ." He stopped as he saw her determined expression. "I have no choice, do I? I must surrender you to the sky and the winds if I am to keep you at all."

She gathered his strong hand in both of hers

and raised it to brush the palm with her lips. "You won't be sorry. I may not always be here when you want me, but I will always be here for you when you need me."

And so Darius had his goldsmith put on the gold backing of the pearl clasp a special mark. It was two intertwining circles, without beginning or end, and symbolized Darius's and Sharah's eternal love for each other.

And for the rest of Darius's life, Sharah came and went from the palace at will. It was reported that at his death, Sharah, wearing her lover's pearls, was by his bedside. Then she and the pearls disappeared, never to be seen again at the court of the Persians. But the story of their love and the pearls was told far and wide until it grew into legend.

One

Someone was following her.

Raine Bennett pulled her long cape tighter around her body and fought back the panic she could feel rising in her chest. The fog hadn't been this bad when she had left her flat in Belgravia. But as she had walked through Green Park, thick fog closed around her, enshrouding her in wet, gray gauze. She'd taken this same path across the park hundreds of times, but tonight all the familiar guideposts were obscured. The trees formed a canopy, holding in the fog. The lights in the lampposts could be seen only as dim, eerily glowing globes. Her field of vision was limited to two steps in front of her, compounding her sense of isolation.

The footsteps behind her seemed to mimic hers with unrelenting threat. She slowed her steps;

the footsteps slowed. She hurried her pace; the footsteps hurried.

She knew that fog magnified sound, yet all she could hear were the footsteps. Raine tried to reason with herself. The person, whoever he was, wasn't following her. It was foolish of her to think that she was the only one crossing the park tonight. She stopped, testing her theory. The footsteps stopped.

She started running. Long, ghostly tendrils of fog wrapped around her, dragging at her, slowing her; fingers of fog covered her face, suffocating her. The footsteps pounded after her. Her heart was hammering so hard she was sure it would burst.

She broke free of the park and the trees, and, too late, saw a big, dark shape coming toward her. She slammed into the shape and screamed.

"What's wrong?" a deep, masculine American voice asked urgently.

Terror-stricken, Raine gasped for breath. Strong hands gripped her arms as she looked up. A streetlamp's light filtered through the gray vapor that was thinner here, allowing her to see a tough-looking face lowered close to hers and light-colored eyes that studied her intently.

"Are you hurt?" Michael asked, tensed, alert.

"I . . ." She listened carefully. The footsteps seemed to be retreating.

"What's wrong? Do you need help?"

"There was someone following me," she managed to say.

"Who?"

With her panic beginning to recede, Raine quickly assessed the big man with whom she had collided. Powerful-looking muscles were laid over his tall, large frame, and his voice was as hard as his face was tough. Strangely, though, she wasn't frightened of him, and she no longer felt isolated. The sense of threat from a stranger in the swirling fog had turned to a sense of intimacy with this stranger. "I don't know who it was. I—"

"Just take it easy," he said, his voice softer now. He eased the pressure of his hands on her arms, but he could still feel the tremors running through her slender body. "I've learned how a London fog can play tricks with your mind. A sound that's two blocks away can seem to come from right over your shoulder."

"Of course, you're right." Unable to help herself, she half-turned and glanced back toward the park. The thick, dank grayness prevented her from seeing anything, but the footsteps had disappeared. Suddenly, weak with relief, she slumped against the man, sheltered by his strong body. "I apologize for careening into you," she murmured, her face pressed into his broad, trench coat—covered chest. "I've lived most of my life in London, and I should be accustomed to weather like this by now."

He stroked her back, noting that her tremors were easing. "There's no need to apologize. Tonight's fog is one of the worst I've ever seen."

She heard his words rumble in his chest, and had the odd urge to use his warmth and strength as she would a downy quilt and pull him around her. But in the few short moments she'd been with him, she'd already realized that while he might protect, he would also unsettle. She drew in a deep breath and inhaled a singularly masculine undertone of musk that combined with a delicious smell of tangy spices and hit her senses with the force of a narcotic. Taken aback by her unusual reaction to him, she pulled slowly away.

He had felt the tension in her body change. If she was confused, he wasn't. Now that he knew there was no danger, he studied her in the dim light. Pale blond hair spilled out of the hood of her lavender cashmere cape, framing a delicately beautiful face. Even through the cape, he sensed the curves that lay beneath. And her eyes were the color of silver rain.

Her purse had been knocked from her arm at the collision and lay open on the ground. She stooped to pick up the scattered contents.

He came down beside her. "What are we looking for?"

"I can't remember everything. There's a compact, comb, handkerchief, change purse—"

"Lipstick?" He held up a slim, golden tube.

Incredibly, the sight of the small, essentially feminine object being held in the hand of someone so inherently masculine struck Raine as provocative. She nodded mutely, and he dropped the lipstick into her purse.

Their hands brushed, and warmth coursed.

Abruptly, Raine rose to her feet. "I think that must be all."

"Are you sure?" he asked, standing also.

"Yes. I appreciate your help, but please don't let me keep you."

"Keep me," he countered, his body very close to her. "I've never seen rain-colored eyes before."

Her heart slammed against her ribs in a different fashion now. Excitement had replaced fear. "I'm meeting friends at the Ritz just across the way. They'll be expecting me."

"For dinner?"

"Drinks. And then we have a charity function to attend afterward." She had given him her schedule for the evening to ward off the expected dinner invitation. It never materialized.

"I'll walk you to the hotel."

"Oh, no, I couldn't ask—"

"As I recall, you didn't ask. I volunteered. Besides, protecting beautiful young women is my specialty."

His tone carried gentle humor, but she could well believe that women were his specialty. In his case, nature had combined its best forces to create a rawly masculine, compellingly sensual man.

"My name is Michael Carr," he said.

"I'm Raine Bennett."

His quick grin took her by surprise as did his next words.

"Your name matches your eyes."

"They're just gray."

"They're *just* beautiful." He touched a finger to

a pale wave of hair that lay by the side of her face. "And so are you."

The unexpected compliment left her speechless. And when he offered her his arm, she took it. As they walked, she said, "You're very American."

He grinned. "That's a compliment, of course."

She couldn't help but return his grin. "It's very American of you to consider it a compliment."

He laughed. "What were you doing in the park all alone?"

"I often cross it at night. Usually, though, it's filled with other people." They were across the street now, and she threw him a curious glance. "What were you doing in the park?"

"I was just out for a walk. The fog was more than I bargained for, though." The lie came easily, perhaps too easily, he thought. In truth, the fog had provided excellent cover for his meeting with Nigel.

"Do you live here in London?"

"No, I'm here on business, working with several English companies to adapt my company's computer systems to their needs." He had given her the standard cover before he realized he was doing it, and the vaguely disturbing idea crossed his mind that clear gray eyes should never be told lies.

"Will you be here long?"

He hesitated. "I'm not sure." That at least was the truth. He nodded to the doorman and accompanied her into the hotel.

She came to a halt beneath an elaborate chandelier and pushed the hood off her head, unaware of the light that refracted from the myriad crystal drops and turned her hair a paler shade of gold. She could see clearly now that his eyes were a penetrating shade of ice blue, and she noticed that a loose swath of his tan-colored hair had fallen over one brow. The urge to reach up and comb her fingers through it came as a surprise to her. She waited until the urge passed, then extended her hand to him. "Thank you for escorting me."

Her hand was swallowed up by both of his. "It was my pleasure," he said. Now that she was no longer frightened, she had retreated behind a wall of cool reserve, but he wasn't put off. When he had closed his arms around her in the park, she had felt soft and vulnerable. When he had inhaled her scent, she had smelled feminine, fascinating, and desirable. Now was not the right time for him to become involved in a relationship, but Raine Bennett had run out of the fog and into his senses. He wanted to spend time with her, to get to know her better. And most of all, he wanted to pull her to him and kiss away her aloof formality.

She didn't like the erratic way her pulses were jumping. She needed to extract her hand from his grasp and walk away, but she couldn't decide how . . . or when. Which was odd, because she couldn't remember the last time she had been uncertain in a social situation. "I hope you enjoy your stay in London."

His blue eyes glittered with an amusement and warmth that made heat rush through her.

"Thank you, I'm sure I will."

"Good-bye."

He didn't say anything, and hesitating only briefly, she turned and walked down the apricot, cream, and dusty rose Long Gallery toward the Palm Court.

Giving her a minute's lead time, Michael shrugged out of his Burberry and slung it over his arm. He was a man who by occupation had to be cautious, but he also frequently relied on instinct. He couldn't explain why he didn't just leave as she clearly expected him to do. He simply knew he had no intention of doing so.

Something about her drew him, and he followed.

He allowed a waiter to settle him at a table that provided an excellent view of her. A man about her age had risen and was helping her out of her cape. Another young woman sat at the table, laughing up at them.

With Raine's back to him and her cape off, Michael could see that her hair was long enough to fall past her shoulders. Her dress spoke of a top designer and was a soft haze of mauve, orchid, and lavender—the bodice a sequined floral pattern, the skirt a billow of plaid silk taffeta. As she leaned toward the seated woman, he got a glimpse of the mauve organza underskirt beneath the plaid silk. The idea that she had money didn't surprise him. She had a certain well-bred polish and sophistication that had already told him she was of the British upper crust, perhaps even to the manner born.

Unconcerned by the thought, he sipped his scotch and waited. The man with Raine handed the hovering waiter her cape, then pulled out a chair. She turned so that she was facing in Michael's direction and sat down.

It was then that he saw the long rope of pearls she was wearing. The large, perfectly matched pearls spilled down the front of her dress, their pink blush gleaming with breathtaking beauty.

He felt as though he'd been kicked in the gut.

He emptied the contents of his glass with one long swallow, signaled for another drink, all the while silently cursing. The one woman in London who could make his blood heat with a mere look from a pair of cool, rain-colored eyes, and she had to be wearing the Pearls of Sharah.

This was going to be complicated.

Lady Pamela Conran threw up her hands in despair at her old boarding school roomie. "I don't understand why you won't tell me where you got that fabulous necklace. If the pearls are real, then please tell me that some wonderfully mysterious, terribly exciting billionaire gave them to you. If they're not real, then tell me where I can get dozens of necklaces just like yours so I can use them in my next collection."

Pamela was a designer whose bright, lively fashions had begun to attract attention. Raine merely smiled. "I borrowed it from a friend, and that's all you need to know."

"If you don't tell me, I'll jump off the Tower Bridge."

Raine was quite used to her friend's theatrics. "You will tell us when, won't you? Edward and I insist on giving you a nice going away party."

"Raine—"

"Edward, change the subject for me."

Viscount Edward Willoughby reached for his drink. "Beastly weather."

"Thank you, Edward," she said dryly.

Having known Raine for so many years, Pamela recognized defeat at overcoming her refusal to talk, and decided to change the subject to something even more interesting than the pearl necklace. She sat forward in her chair and leaned confidentially toward Raine. "Darling, are you aware that there is a perfectly smashing-looking man four tables over who's been staring at you ever since you sat down?"

Raine nodded and reached for her wineglass.

"Really?" Pamela looked at her friend with new interest. "Then I don't know how you're managing to stay so calm. He's positively the sexiest man I've seen in ages. With one look I'm sure he could wipe the serenity from the Mona Lisa's face and replace it with lust."

Raine privately agreed. Michael had such presence, she hadn't needed to glance his way again, after first seeing him there, to know that he was staring at her.

"And look at the way he wears his clothes. Elegant, but with a maddening casualness. That's a Perry Ellis jacket he has on. The texture of the fabric makes you want to touch. Or maybe it's the *man* that makes you want to touch." She gave a delicate shudder. "Lord, Raine, if it were me he was staring at like that, I'd be a blob of custard."

"That's because you're incredibly fast," Edward said.

Pamela wrinkled her nose at him. "I'm not at all fast." After some thought, she added, "I'm simply open to options."

"Is that what they're calling it these days?"

Raine listened with half an ear to the familiar sound of her friends' bickering. When she had been ten years old, her parents had divorced, leaving her feeling lonely and confused. Over a long weekend from school, Pamela had taken her home and introduced her to the young boy who lived on the neighboring estate. The three of them had been the best of friends ever since.

Pamela reached across the table and smacked Edward's hand. "I really hate it when you act so supercilious. You never used to, you know. I think it's the influence of that crowd you've been running with."

Edward's patrician features showed a need to correct her. "It seems to me that I'm running with you and Raine."

"You condescended to meet us for drinks before the ball. When's the last time we've seen you, *really* seen you?"

Raine bent her head and studied the amber liquid in her glass. She was finding Michael's fixed ice-blue stare terribly disconcerting. She didn't think she'd ever had a man look at her with such potent concentration. But then, Michael seemed different from any man she'd ever known. Sitting perfectly still, he emanated an incredible energy and power that she could feel halfway across the room. And at the moment she seemed to be the recipient of the total sum of his intensity.

"Raine, when are you going to quit your dreary courier job and come to work for me?" Pamela asked.

Raine blinked. Evidently, the conversation had changed once more. "Work for you doing what? I can barely manage to put in a hem."

"As a model, for heaven's sake! That tall, slender body of yours would be perfect to show off my clothes."

Edward groaned. "Not even Raine's fair beauty could make your stuff look good."

Pamela hit him again. "What are you talking about? I've sold two evening gowns and one day frock to the Princess of Wales. Already she's worn one of the evening gowns, and I understand the gown created quite a flurry."

"I hope it wasn't that spangled chartreuse."

Pamela subsided. "You always remember my mistakes."

For the first time that evening, he chuckled. "I'm sorry. It's just that I can't forget some of the numbers you ran up for your dolls."

"Some of those dresses were wonderful, ahead of their time even." She turned to Raine. "For heaven's sake, tell me who he is."

"Who?" she asked, knowing exactly to whom Pamela was referring.

"*Him.* Lord, but he looks dangerous. Like a big cat plunked down among the marble columns and gilt of this Edwardian-style room. *Raine,* who *is* he?"

Refusing to glance toward Michael, Raine conjured an image of him in her mind. Big, tough, with ice-blue eyes that could make her feel heat. Dangerous? Oh, yes. But for a few minutes in the park he had seemed an island of safety. "He's an American I met as I was coming across Green Park. The fog was unnerving me, and he was kind enough to walk me here."

"Really?" Pamela's eyes lighted. "Well, let's call him over for a drink. I'd love to meet him."

Raine grabbed Pamela's hand just as it was about to signal Michael. "*No.* In fact—you know what?—I just realized I'm rather tired. I think I'll go home."

Edward was jolted out of his malaise. "What? But it's early yet. And there's the ball . . ."

"Suddenly I'm not in the mood. You two go and have fun, and be loves and give everyone my regrets."

"Aren't you feeling well?" Pamela asked with concern.

"I'm fine. It's just as I said. I'm a little tired, and I'd rather avoid the crush of the ball if I can."

"I can think of at least two men," Pamela said, "maybe three if you count Randall James Nicholas, which I never do, marquess though he may be, who are going to be very disappointed."

Raine shrugged. "They'll understand. Tell them I developed a headache and decided to go home. Besides, I just remembered, I'm working tomorrow. I should never have even come out tonight."

Pamela's look was clearly dubious. "Since when have you been bothered by late hours?"

Raine ignored her. "Will you be in to work tomorrow, Edward?"

"You know I don't enjoy working as much as you do. I take assignments only when I'm out of fun funds."

Raine's grin was filled with affection. "That's right, it's the first of the month, isn't it? You've gotten your allowance. In that case, you can pay for our drinks."

"In that case," Pamela said, catching the eye of their waiter, "I'll have another."

Raine stood but bent back down to drop a kiss on Pamela's cheek. "Take care. I'll talk to you soon." Edward had risen, and she brushed his cheek with her lips. "When will I see you again?"

"In about a week," he said cheerfully, "when I've spent this month's allowance."

"I worry about you sometimes," she whispered.

"Don't. I'm fine, really."

"All right, then. Ring if you need me."

• • •

Raine pulled the hood of her cape over her hair and gazed in the direction of the park. The fog seemed just as thick as it had an hour earlier, and she decided she would definitely take a taxi. But, amazingly, before she could move to signal the doorman, before Michael even spoke, she felt his presence behind her.

"You decided not to go to the ball?" Michael asked.

She turned slowly toward him, her pulses racing. "Yes."

"I'm glad, and I think we should take a taxi, don't you?" He flipped up the collar of his trench coat and signaled the doorman.

"We?"

"Unless you'd like to walk?" he said.

His quick grin appeared before she was ready for it, making her heart miss a beat. "I can see myself home."

"I know. But I'd like to make sure you get there safely." Unexpectedly, he reached out to adjust the hood around her face, then he brushed her cheek lightly with a finger.

He was so big, she thought, yet his touch was so gentle. "I'd rather you didn't."

"Why?"

"I'm accustomed to seeing myself home."

"That's a real pity." He took her arm and started to lead her toward the taxi that was waiting for them. "Where do you live?"

She jerked her arm out of his grasp, stopped where she was, and gazed at him with wonder. "You're like a tidal wave, sweeping people along in your wake. Is it because you're so big or because you're an American?"

"It's because I've never learned to take no for an answer." He paused as he suddenly saw the reluctance in her eyes, the reluctance any woman would have about inviting a man she barely knew back to her flat. "Raine, if I'd wanted to do you harm, I could have pushed you back into the park and done whatever I wanted."

"I know." She honestly didn't think he meant her any physical harm. But something was telling her that he could well represent a different, perhaps even more insidious kind of danger than the footsteps in the park had.

"I'll stay only a short time," he promised softly. "I'll even tell the taxi to come back for me in thirty minutes. That will give us time to have a drink."

One fine brow arched. "You think I'm going to invite you in?"

"Aren't you?"

"You're very sure of yourself."

"If you mean that I know what I want, then you're right."

She yielded to the tidal wave of his charm and forceful personality. "Thirty minutes, Michael Carr. No more."

He grinned. "Where do you live?"

"I have a flat just across the park in Belgravia," she said, and gave him the address.

•   •   •

Her apartment was quietly elegant and understated. "Do you have a job?" he asked, looking around as he unbelted his Burberry and shrugged out of it.

She smiled, amused at his obvious train of thought. "Yes, I work for the London Express Service, transporting documents and reports too sensitive to be trusted to mail, machine, or any other form of communication."

His head came up, like an animal sensing danger. "You're a courier?"

She was already turning and missed his reaction. "Yes. Make yourself comfortable, and I'll get our drinks."

When she disappeared through a doorway, he let out a soft string of expletives. *He'd been set up.* It was the only explanation he could come up with. In his world nothing was ever simple or coincidental: A beautiful woman, wearing a rope of pearls he knew had been recently stolen, and working for a courier company, had collided with him in the fog. It couldn't have been an accident, he thought.

But why? What was going on? And where in the hell did Raine Bennett fit in?

He reviewed his options but quickly decided he didn't have any. Truthfully, he didn't *want* any other than staying close to Raine.

He walked around the room, taking in the ambience with which she surrounded herself, looking for something, anything, that might explain Raine Bennett to him. What he saw stirred his senses. She had mixed fabrics—chintz, velvet, silk, lace—in a way that was richly sensual, and, he decided on the spot, uniquely her. Patterns were gentle, and the colors ranged from candlelight to pale green to mauve and provided light and softness. In one corner antique enameled boxes enlivened a circular walnut table.

He committed the number on the telephone dial to memory, then continued on around the room. There was potpourri in delicate china bowls, the latest best-seller on the coffee table.

On the white marble mantel he found two silver-framed pictures. One picture was of a distinguished older man. He had dark brown hair with wings of silver at his temples and a mustache above his well-shaped mouth.

"My father," she said, just coming back into the room, "and the other picture is of my mother." Her hands held filled crystal tumblers.

He threw a glance at the second silver-framed photograph and saw an attractive woman with blond hair the color of Raine's. "Do your parents live nearby?"

"My father lives in St. James. My mother lives in America. Kentucky, actually."

"An American?"

She handed him a drink with a smile. "Technically speaking, I'm half American, but I feel ninety-nine point nine percent British. I've spent most of my life right here in England, you see."

"Why was that?"

"My mother's family has raised horses in Kentucky for generations. When my parents divorced, my mother returned home, and for a while I tried living there too."

Okay, he thought, the money could come from Kentucky. He wanted very much to believe it did.

"But . . ." A shadow passed over her face.

"But?" he prompted.

"I'm afraid of horses."

The way she said it, as if she were admitting some terrible secret, made him chuckle. Suddenly he wanted to take her into his arms and kiss her and tell her she'd never have to go near another horse as long as she lived. But he didn't, because she was wearing a stolen necklace. And she worked as a courier. And he couldn't decide whether her clear gray eyes were lying. Or whether he cared much if they were.

"When I was a little girl, the horse I was riding went down and nearly crushed me. When I fell, I dropped into a ravine, and he rolled right over me. I was knocked unconscious. Fortunately, though, I came out of it with only a few bruises. A day later my mother insisted that I climb right back on another horse. I was scared to death, but I didn't want to seem a coward, so I did it anyway."

"What happened?"

"The horse bolted and ran away with me. I've never been on a horse since."

He smiled. "You sound embarrassed."

"When you are one of the Thornegoods of Kentucky, it is not considered good form to be afraid of horses. In Kentucky I'm spoken of in whispers."

"I don't believe it."

"I'm afraid so." It came as a shock to realize that she was enjoying herself. She had spent the last six years avoiding any man who showed the slightest sexual interest in her, and there was no doubt that Michael's interest in her was sexual. Yet she was actually relaxed with him.

"How does your father view this terrible maladjustment of yours?"

Her face softened. "My father blames all horses, everywhere, for my fear. And even though he grew up around horses, he hasn't ridden since out of loyalty to me."

"You're close, then?" he asked. He felt frustrated. While she was telling him things about herself, she wasn't giving him information that was proving helpful to him. Of course, the fault could lie with his questions, he thought with a bleak humor aimed directly at himself. He couldn't seem to overcome his desire to be gentle with her.

Raine thought about the term "close" and decided it did and it didn't apply to her and her father. Her father was the most eccentric person she knew, and one of his eccentricities was that their relationship remain private. "My father and I adore each other," she finally said, "but we live very separate lives. Different friends, different pastimes. How is your scotch?"

"Excellent." He set the crystal tumbler on the mantel and went to her. The man within him wanted to kiss her. The professional within him wanted to find out what the hell she was doing with those pearls and why she had run into him in the fog. Until he reached her, he didn't know what he would do.

"I'm going to kiss you," he said, and lowered his mouth to hers.

For just a moment she held herself tense, then with a sigh he found exquisite she went weak against him. She tasted the way she smelled, he thought. Richly feminine, infinitely fascinating, and desirable as hell. She made him want her so badly, his bones were hurting.

Surprising them both, he ended the kiss.

With his chest heaving, he lifted his head and gazed down at her. In his arms she was all sequins and silk, heat and soft passion. She was quivering against him, her rain-colored eyes velvety with desire; and, unwilling to break contact with her entirely, he rubbed the smooth skin of her neck. He had to concentrate on what was important . . . except some hard-to-control feeling was telling him it was *she* who was important, and nothing or no one else. He took a deep breath and tried to harden himself against the enticement of her allure. "Your necklace is lovely. Was it a gift?"

She was clinging to his broad shoulders, but at his question she ran her tongue over her bottom lip, and her eyes turned vaguely confused. "It's not mine," she said, her voice still whispery with arousal. "I, uh, borrowed it. From a friend."

His suspicion of her deepened, but his need for her did not die. His mind stayed cool, but his body was burning for her. He threaded his fingers into her hair and pulled her back to him for another kiss.

He was angry about something, she realized, but she had no idea about what. His anger bewildered her, but not as much as the passion he stirred in her. Since Philip's death, there had been other men who had kissed her, asking, pleading without words for her to show them that she felt something. Michael neither asked nor pleaded. He demanded, and he received. Her response to him frightened her. Years of control shouldn't crumble that easily. She pushed away and put distance between them.

"I want to see you tomorrow," he said in a low, rough whisper.

"No, I'm working."

"After work."

"No." She folded her hands together to still their unsteadiness, and walked to the fireplace. "Please go."

"Tell me something, Raine." The irregular edges had been cleared from his voice now, leaving only a smooth, casual curiosity. "Does this cool, haughty act of yours scare off other men?"

"I don't know what you mean."

"I *mean*, you put up signs that say *stay away, keep off, don't touch.* I just want to know if it works with other men"—he crossed the room to her and pressed a hard, fierce kiss to her lips—

"because, honey, it sure as hell does not work with me." He kissed her again, only this time with gentleness that flooded her with a delicious, sweet warmth. "Good night, Raine. I'll see you tomorrow."

He stood on the street outside her flat and looked up at the lighted windows of her sitting room and thought of the way her rain-colored eyes had turned soft when he kissed her. Dammit! Why did she have to smell and feel like every fantasy he'd ever had?

This was going to be extremely complicated.

Two

Raine took off the pearls and placed them carefully in their box. Then she shoved the box to the far back corner of the top shelf in her closet. Perhaps she shouldn't have worn the pearls tonight, she thought. She'd never done anything like that before—taken and worn something that wasn't hers—but somehow the loveliness of the pearls had proved irresistible, and she hadn't thought it would hurt this once.

Succumbing to temptation was very unlike her—just as succumbing to the charms of Michael Carr had been. He said he'd never learned to take no for an answer, and no was the only answer she ever gave to a man. She considered herself a strong woman with her life fully under control, but a controlled life could easily be destroyed by the force of a tidal wave. . . .

The ringing of her doorbell broke into her thoughts. She threw a glance at her clock and saw that it was a bit after midnight. Michael had been gone only five minutes. Had he come back? Despite herself, her step was quick as she hurried to the door, her evening gown rustling around her.

She opened the door, and an emotion that came perilously close to disappointment washed through her as she eyed the man dressed in evening clothes who was standing on the threshold.

"Father, what are you doing here this late?"

Lord Reginald St. Clair strolled in, very much the dapper man-about-town, a tightly furled umbrella perched jauntily on his shoulder, a large box under his arm. "Hello, darling. You look lovely, although I must say I'm glad you decided not to attend the ball, and, I might add, I'm especially glad that your new beau didn't stay long. Big chap, isn't he?"

"You mean you've been waiting outside?" she asked, walking ahead of him down the hall and into the sitting room.

"Well, I had to drop off this." He took the box out from under his arm and placed it casually on a side table.

She eyed the box with resignation. How many years had her father been purchasing art objects and jewels with his gambling earnings and bringing them to her to keep. "What is it this time?"

"Just a little Gauguin sculpture I picked up. Keep it for me, won't you, darling? When I need the funds, I'll come for it. And as usual, this will remain our little secret."

"Father, why do you insist on buying these things with your winnings and having me keep them for you? Why don't you put your money in the bank like everyone else?"

"The appreciation in value of art and jewels over time is much greater than the interest the bank offers." His dark eyes twinkled with mischief. "Anyway, if my funds were that liquid, I'd spend them, now, wouldn't I? Look at how quickly I went through your mother's settlement to me."

"That was extraordinary," Raine agreed.

"Besides, money in the bank is too available for the tax man."

"Father, you are a peer of the realm."

"The realm has my unfaltering allegiance. It does not need my fluctuating funds."

"You know if you need money, all you have to do is ask."

"Your grandmother Thornegood's fortune was left to you, my darling, not to me. And God knows, you certainly earned the Bennett money." At the sight of furrows in her brow, he leaned forward and kissed her cheek. "Don't fret. You know I have my principles, and I will not take money from my daughter."

She sighed and, mentally putting aside the topic for another day, she took in his evening attire. "Are you heading home or just going out?"

"Actually, I thought I'd pop into one of the clubs before calling it a night."

"Father, I wish you'd find some other way of supporting yourself besides gambling. I worry about you."

"Gentlemen have been gambling since the dawn of time, Raine. Besides, it's the only thing I was ever trained to do. My father, your grandfather, the twelfth Baron St. Clair, taught me cards when I was still in short pants."

"Why couldn't he have taught you investment banking, I wonder."

"Because card playing was all he knew. The family fortune started dwindling with him, I'm afraid. He did, however, give me one piece of advice I will always thank him for."

"What's that?"

"Marry an heiress, he said. And I did. And look what I got for it. You, my love." He stroked her cheek, his touch gentle with love.

Suddenly she had had her fill for the evening of persuasive, forceful men who could wrap her around their little fingers with no effort at all. "You have too much charm and not enough sense, Father."

Reginald studied her thoughtfully. "My, you're very cross tonight. What's wrong?"

She sighed. "I guess I'm just tired."

Immediately, he looked repentant. "I'm sorry to stop by so late, but I did try to see you earlier this evening."

"When?"

"In the park. I tried to catch up to you."

"That was *you* who was following me?"

He raised a brow as if he were surprised she should think it had been anyone else. "Of course."

"For goodness' sake, *why* all the stealth?"

"Darling, you know how I insist on our affairs being private. I didn't want anyone to see me giving you my latest acquisition. And when you met up with that chap, I decided to wait until later." He gave her a satisfied smile as if to say, look how well things turned out.

She groaned. "You nearly scared me out of ten years of my life."

"I'm sorry, darling. I didn't realize."

Her lips curved into a rueful smile. "I've never been able to stay angry at you for long, have I? Never mind. No harm done."

She thought of Michael Carr. *No harm done?* She fervently hoped not.

In his room in the small hotel located in the heart of Mayfair, Michael placed a call to Paris. "My meeting with Nigel went off without a hitch, but so far he's having no luck at getting any hard evidence against Clinton Ayers." He paused, listening. "Well, we may have gotten a break. I met a woman tonight, and she was wearing the Pearls of Sharah. I recognized it from the fax description you sent me a few days ago."

He listened for a moment. "Yes, it's the same necklace that was stolen from Ayers and has him out of his mind with fury. I still think his rabid reaction to the necklace's theft will be of help to us. It will give us a good opportunity to watch his organization in action, plus it's just possible he will be so distracted by his efforts to get the pearls back that he will get careless."

Another pause. "I'm not sure what to think about her. It's like I'm seeing two different sides of a coin at the same time, and I can't decide which side should be turned up.

"Our meeting appeared to be accidental. And she seems too intelligent to be wearing in public a piece of jewelry she knows is stolen. Still . . . the only time the necklace was exposed was in the Ritz bar, and then only for about an hour. If she and the necklace were set up as some sort of lure for me, then it was very successful.

"Oh, and there's one more thing. She works as a courier for the London Express Service." He listened, and his expression turned even more grim than it had been. "I know, and don't worry. I plan to stay very close to her."

Cameron McSheeney glanced at the foot-high pile of papers on his desk, mentally shrugged, and turned his gaze toward Raine. She was much easier on the eyes, he concluded. This morning she was wearing a smart little suit with a short, flirty dove-gray skirt, a pale pink silk blouse, and a loose, cream-colored, three-quarter-length linen jacket. The outfit probably cost more than he made in a week, he thought ruefully, but he no longer questioned why a beautiful young heiress would want to work as a courier. He simply accepted with gratitude the fact that she did.

Raine worked three days a week, plus she took on any special assignments for which he might need her. He supposed from her point of view, this part-time job gave her a sense of purpose, along with the charity services she performed, and the courier work was certainly anything but routine. From the company's viewpoint, young bluebloods such as Raine and Viscount Edward Willoughby—on those rare days when he deigned to appear—made the perfect couriers. No one would suspect that the leather folders, briefcases, or gift-wrapped packages they carried contained top secret papers. And in these times, when courier thefts were on the rise, he'd take any advantage he could get.

"I have a special errand for you today."

"What is it?" Raine was used to getting "special" jobs. She was aware that her appearance made her valuable to the company.

"Well, this one's a bit unusual, but it came from the chairman himself."

Raine narrowed her eyes on Cameron. "Why do you sound so hesitant?"

He rubbed at his temple with a forefinger. "I told you it was a bit unusual." He grimaced before continuing. "The instructions are these: you're to go to Fortnum and Mason's, pick up a hamper—"

"A hamper?"

"A hamper. Outside of Fortnum and Mason's

there will be a car and a driver. He will take you to the destination."

"This is a joke, surely?"

Cameron shook his head. "No, it is not a joke, and it is definitely on the up and up. The chairman assured me."

"Get someone else."

"You were specifically requested."

Raine rose from her chair and went to stand by the window, her mind filled with the name of Michael Carr. Could he possibly be behind this? Strange that she should think of him. Or was it? She had no idea where he was at this moment, but she could almost feel him like a tangible presence near her. She shivered and told herself that she was imagining things. His effect on her had been powerful, but she had to forget their encounter and get on with her life. Still, equal parts of excitement and apprehension settled in the pit of her stomach and refused to go away.

"Raine?"

"All right, Cameron. I'll do it."

Her excitement and apprehension grew as she accepted what was clearly a picnic hamper from the frock-coated shopwalker in Fortnum and Mason's, then made her way outside to find a Rolls-Royce and a liveried chauffeur. The car drove northwest, away from the curious mix of the diesel-and-springtime smell of the city. It wasn't long before she realized that they were heading toward the vast stretch of parkland high on a hill above London. Hampstead Heath. It was a perfect place for a picnic. And she had the hamper.

When the car pulled to a stop and she got out, she wasn't at all surprised to see Michael waiting for her.

A welcoming grin on his face, a blanket under his arm, he reached for the picnic hamper. "You made it. Great. I hope you didn't have any trouble."

"I'm not staying."

"Nonsense." He waved at the chauffeur, then motioned to the sky. "The fog is gone. The sun is out. The air is clear and warm. And, as it happens, it's time for lunch."

"Michael—"

Behind her, she heard the car drive away, and she looked at him with accusation. He smiled down at her. "I don't take no for an answer, remember? Come on, let's find a nice square of grass. One of the things I've always admired about England is the grass. It's *so* green. It's as if England has been working on its lawns for hundreds of years." The humorous gleam in his eyes invited her to enjoy his joke.

She could have protested. She could have refused to go with him. There were people around them, and he wouldn't drag her to a picnic spot against her will. Or, she amended, she didn't think he would. The excitement in her stomach was fast overtaking her apprehension. And, she discovered, she was hungry.

Last night she uncharacteristically had allowed

the beauty of the pearls to entice her into wearing them. Then she had met Michael. And ever since, his compelling magnetism had been slowly, relentlessly, pulling at her, luring her into doing something she'd vowed she would never do again: feel something besides friendship for a man.

She was still fighting the feelings growing inside her, but she wasn't sure she should. The heat and happiness felt too good. Perhaps after all these years it would be all right. Perhaps it was time to try again.

But she should proceed cautiously, she told herself, until she knew for sure. In the meantime it wouldn't hurt to relax the hold on her emotions a little.

She smiled at him, and Michael's pulse jerked. What had just happened? Her wall of reserve had come tumbling down right before his eyes, he realized with astonishment. It was what he'd wanted, but while the man in him was intrigued, the professional in him was suspicious. Somehow he had to satisfy both sides of himself.

Michael stopped on a hill thick with grass and backed by trees. He eyed the postcard view of London with satisfaction, then took one last look to make sure they were well away from other visitors to the heath. "This spot looks nice." He snapped the blanket free of its folds, spread it over the cushiony grass, and sat down. "Make yourself comfortable, and I'll serve you."

Raine kicked off her high-heeled pumps, slipped

out of her jacket, and settled onto the blanket, facing him.

With the sun and the wind in her pale hair, she looked young, innocent, and very beautiful. Her pale pink silk blouse gently skimmed the curves of her breasts. The short skirt rose above her knees as she shifted her legs to one side and braced herself on her arm. It took an effort to force his thoughts away from how sexy she was. "You didn't wear your necklace today?"

She cast him an odd look. "I told you it wasn't mine."

"Oh, that's right. I forgot." He reached for the hamper and lifted its lid. "Well, I guess, in any event, you wouldn't wear it while you were working. Being a courier must be an interesting job, carrying around important documents that represent millions of dollars."

For some reason she found herself annoyed by what he said. Maybe, she decided, it was the purpose she had thought she'd heard beneath his casual tone. Her gray eyes cooled visibly. "Oh, dear, I'm afraid something has blown onto the shoulder of your jacket."

He looked at his shoulder and saw a bit of lint. He shrugged out of the jacket and laid it aside. "You know, the English have the most polite way of ignoring questions, and I find it both charming and maddening."

One fair, aristocratic brow arched. "Really? Did you ask me a question?"

His grin was quick and left her breathless. "I intended to. I guess I didn't, though."

She tilted her head, and sunshine caught and tangled in the long, gently waving strands of her hair. "Who are you, Michael Carr?"

He paused in the act of unstrapping two plates from the hamper's lid. "You know who I am. You just said my name, and I told you last night that I'm in London on business." His blue eyes sharpened. "What's bothering you, Raine? I mean beside the obvious, that you're here against your will."

"I'm not here against my will. I'm perfectly capable of hiking back down the hill and calling a taxi."

He rested an arm on an upraised knee. "Then what's bothering you?"

The softness of his voice made warmth shiver through her. She waited a beat for the feeling to pass. "I want to know how you arranged this. Fortnum and Mason's and Hampstead Heath are not exactly the London Express Service's usual line."

"Raine, you should know you can arrange anything if you want to badly enough."

"Then you must be very rich."

"Not particularly. I'm just very determined. We're having chili dogs. I hope you like them." He delved into the hamper and brought out an insulated container. "With freshly made New Mexico chili."

"Freshly made chili? From Fortnum and Mason's?"

"Very early this morning I made the acquaintance of that good establishment's chef. He whipped this up for us from my own recipe."

She thought of the delicate cakes, tea sandwiches, and biscuits that the chef usually made. "I can't even imagine . . . he must have been appalled."

"I paid him a great deal of money not to be appalled."

She smiled in spite of herself. "You're trying to impress me, aren't you?"

He took her question seriously, gazing fixedly at her in an unsettling way. "Yes. Is it working?"

"I'm not sure." She told the truth. She didn't know what to make of this covert assignation on the heath or the man who had arranged it. She knew only that she was feeling strong, heated emotions for the first time in years, and whether it was good or bad remained to be seen.

"What does impress you?"

She made up her mind suddenly. *You*, she thought. But she asked, "What else have you got there?"

He held her gaze, keeping her on the hook a moment longer, then he turned to the hamper and pulled out several more containers. "These are our hot dogs. Well, actually, they're English sausages, but they were the best we could do on short notice. And the chef made up special buns for us." He held up what looked like a roll to her. "Hot dog buns," he said, and pulled out a last, padded insulated container. "Beer. We'll need it to cool the taste of the spicy chili."

"Did you say *New Mexico* chili?"

He nodded, putting together a chili dog and setting it on a plate to the side of her where it wasn't between them but could easily be reached. "That's where I'm from. Ever been there?"

"No." She eyed the chili dog hesitantly. "Spicy?"

"Extremely." He popped the caps on the two beers and set hers by her plate. "And, by the way, the idea is to eat it, not just look at it."

"Where are the forks?"

He chuckled and picked up the chili dog with a big hand and brought it to her mouth. "This is definitely finger food."

She took a bite, and he watched her closely. "Why are you making that face?"

"I wasn't making a face. It's just that it's not like anything I've ever tasted before."

He took a bite and made a similar face. "It's not exactly like back home."

He looked so perturbed, she laughed out loud. "It's fine, really."

He dumped the chili dog onto the plate. "You have the loveliest skin, absolutely flawless."

Her laughter fled at his sudden change of subject, and she gazed at him, bothered. "You never told me who you are."

"It's simple, Raine. I'm someone who wants you very much."

The heat sprang up out of nowhere. She pushed

it down, picked up the chili dog, and took another bite. "So you live in New Mexico?"

He took his napkin and wiped a spot of chili off her chin. "No, that's where I grew up. In Albuquerque."

"London must seem very different."

He took a swig of his beer, grateful that she hadn't realized he had omitted telling her where he lived now. Relating his cover story to people had always come easily to him. Raine was proving the exception. He didn't want to lie to her any more than he already had. "Well, let's see. Both cities have rivers running through them. One the Thames, the other the Rio Grande. But, of course, London doesn't have nearly as much sun or desert as Albuquerque does."

Her lips quirked with humor. "No, I guess not."

"And when Christopher Wren was rebuilding London, Indians were still roaming over New Mexico."

"I don't believe London ever had that problem."

He smiled. "I miss waking up in the morning and seeing the sun rise over the mountains. My family still lives there. I have a younger brother and two sisters, all married with kids. My mother's wonderful. By the time I was eleven years old, I was already taller than she, but she still worries and fusses over me as if I were her little boy. She sends me a big box of chocolate chip cookies once a month. And if she doesn't get a call from me once every two weeks, I get an irate letter. I guess all mothers are the same, though."

Raine's expression held no bitterness or resentment. "Not mine. She never fussed over me, even when I was little. Her method of raising a child was roughly akin to how she takes care of her horses."

"That's awful."

"Not really. Very early on I got used to her method and understood that it's the only way she knows. And she takes very good care of her horses. Only the best feed, trainers, and veterinarians. Just like her horses, I received the best of everything."

His gaze was thoughtful. "And she lives in Kentucky with her horses, and you and your father lead separate lives in London. That sounds very lonely."

His remark struck an unexpected nerve. "Not at all. I have a very full life."

"Any brothers or sisters?"

Raine shook her head.

"Husbands, ex-husbands, fiancés, ex-fiancés, someone with whom you're seriously or otherwise involved?"

She met his gaze. "Would it matter?"

"Not in the least."

A thrill gently rippled through her. Trying not to appear as disconcerted as she felt, she nodded toward the hamper. "What else do we have?"

"Chocolate chip cookies made to my mother's recipe, only the chef kept calling them biscuits." He raised a finger and touched the skin exposed by the V of the blouse. "Wouldn't you like to ask me if I'm married or otherwise involved?"

His finger slid leisurely toward the first button of the blouse, trailing heat over her skin. "No," she murmured.

"Why not?"

"Because I'm not sure I would care, and I know I should."

As he had done the night before, he announced his intentions. "I'm going to kiss you." He spread his hands up the sides of her neck and brought his long fingers beneath her hair until he cradled her head. Then he touched her lips very softly. She gasped, and he pulled away slightly. "Relax. It will be all right."

"I'm not sure it will be."

"It's got to be. Lord, Raine, I want to do more than kiss you. Much more." Then he was kissing her again. Slowly, he pushed her back onto the blanket and came down half on top of her.

"Michael." His name came out as a helpless moan.

"Shhh." He took her bottom lip between his teeth and gently pulled. Then he captured her tongue and did the same.

A sweetness and warmth grew low in her stomach. She had often seen young lovers in the parks around the city, kissing and holding each other close; but she had never done anything like that. Not even as a teenager or when she was engaged to Philip. Philip had been much too fastidious for what he would have considered "abandoned" activities.

Raine let the heat flow unchecked.

The cooling breeze wafted over Hampstead Heath, rustling through the treetops, flirting with the daffodils, playing with the hem of Raine's skirt, ruffling Michael's hair.

His big body pressed down on her. He longed to unbutton her blouse, let his hand feel the sweet weight of her breast and his thumb worry at the hardened nipple. He longed to slide his hand beneath her skirt and up to the softness between her legs. He was hard and aching. "I want you," he said, and drove his tongue into her mouth.

Kissing her was so easy. Making love to her would be even easier. The thought made him deepen his kiss, and she responded by wrapping her arms around his neck and holding him close.

He didn't know how long he would have gone on kissing her. Or if he could have refrained from doing more. But gradually, he became aware of distant laughter, and he eased the pressure of his mouth. Then she made a little sound of protest, and he nearly forgot his resolve and lost control. He tore his lips from hers and looked around them. "I heard some voices, but I don't see anyone."

She ran her tongue over her swollen bottom lip. He saw the gesture and touched his finger to the moistness, then slipped his finger between his lips and sucked their combined taste into his mouth.

She shut her eyes against the sensual act.

He came up on an elbow. "Raine . . . let's go back to your flat."

With her eyes still closed, she shook her head.

"Then my hotel."

"No."

"Open your eyes and look at me, Raine." His voice was a gruff whisper. At this moment the professional in him had ceased to exist. He was all man, and he had never wanted a woman the way he wanted Raine Bennett.

Slowly, her lids lifted. "I don't think I should see you again."

He drew in a deep, steadying breath. "Under the circumstances, I don't think you could have said anything more strange."

"You don't understand."

"Obviously. Why don't you explain." He rolled away and sat up, then offered her his hand and helped her into a sitting position. A pale strand of hair had fallen against her cheek; he brushed it back. "I'm waiting."

"I don't trust easily. And I don't know if I can trust you."

The irony of her words almost made him flinch. He had no comeback for her.

"I had a bad marriage. It was six years ago. To Philip Bennett."

"So you're divorced?"

"No, I'm a widow. But if he hadn't crashed on the autobahn during a trip to Germany, I would have divorced him."

Her eyes were fixed on a point beyond his shoulders. He smoothed his fingers through her hair again because he couldn't help himself. "Do you want to tell me about it?"

"No. Not really. But I do want you to understand, so I'll just say that I was very young, very much in love. Philip's courtship was quite romantic and swept me right off my feet. I thought he was wonderful, and to this day I'm convinced that he loved me in his way. But even so, once we were married, he totally ignored me. It took me a while to realize that he wanted me as a prize to put in a glass case where I could only be seen and not touched, especially by him."

"How very, very stupid of the man," he answered.

She shrugged. "Yes, well, I was the stupid one. I couldn't see past my love for him to understand what he really wanted of me."

Guilt stabbed through him. He took her chin and turned her face toward him. Vulnerability clouded her gray eyes and made him wish to hell he was the businessman he had told her he was. But something had started last night in the fog, and it had to be finished. "That was six long years ago. Don't you think it's time to give another man a chance?"

"I think you want more than a chance."

"Have dinner with me tonight. Let's find out together what I want."

"I don't know . . ."

He reached out and circled his fingers around her neck. "I'll make a deal with you. You can break my heart."

Responding to an impulse, Raine pressed the flat of her hand to his heart. Beneath her palm she felt the strong, steady thud. "Your heart can't be broken. It's too big and tough—like you."

A slow smile touched his lips. "I hope you're right."

That night Michael took Raine to dinner at a jazz club in Soho. They ate pasta, drank wine, sat very close together, and stayed long past the time when they should have left, listening to the jazz and staring into each other's eyes.

Later, in the hallway of her flat, he pushed her against the wall, no longer caring if she were involved up to her lovely aristocratic neck with the theft of the pearls or the multicountry industrial espionage organization he was investigating. He had a hunger inside of him for her that was burning him up. She was wearing a dress of fragile layers of ivory silk, almost the same color as her skin. His hands found the silk first, then her skin. Her skin was hot to the touch. He tugged and pulled at the layers of silk until he could fill his hands with her breasts.

Raine's head went back against the wall. There was a tension in her that made her feel as if she were going to snap in two. She knew she couldn't allow this to continue, but maybe for just a few minutes more . . . Her breasts felt full, aching . . . and loved. He wasn't gentle in his caresses, but he wasn't being rough either. He touched her as if it were absolutely right that he do so. She would have slid down the wall if it hadn't been for the pressure of his body. He was holding her upright; he was controlling her every response; he was driving her mad.

"Michael . . . we must—"

"Don't tell me to stop," he said thickly.

Weakly, she pushed against his chest. "I'm not ready."

Abruptly, his hand went under her skirt and skimmed up her inner thigh to the lace edge of her panties. "Do you want me to show you how ready you are?"

"That's not what I meant," she cried, even as she wondered why she was holding back. She wanted him so badly, she felt swamped by the need. Tears clogged her throat, making speaking almost impossible. But to give her heart again was a giant step for her. "Don't you see? I have to make sure . . . I have to make sure that it's really what I want and that it's not just you overwhelming me."

He could have overcome her resistance. He knew it with a certainty that had him shaking. But the sound of her tears stopped him. He stilled against her, and for a moment concentrated on the seemingly impossible act of pulling air into his lungs. Then, inch by painful inch, he straightened away from her. He kept his gaze from her eyes and carefully adjusted her clothing. "I think I'd better leave now."

She bit her bottom lip. "I'm sorry."

"Don't apologize. It's all right. Or, rather, it will be, I suppose." He lay three fingers over the frantically beating pulse at the base of her neck. "Have I told you how much I love your skin? It feels like silk and looks as if it has the consistency of pure cream. Every time I look at it, I have an urge to run my tongue over you, to just lap and lap until I'm full. The problem is, I don't think I could ever get full of you."

Helplessly, she closed her eyes. "Michael . . ."

He tried to clear the constriction from his throat. "Tomorrow night?"

"A friend is having a party. I promised to attend. Come with me?"

He thought of the meeting he had scheduled for the next evening. "I may be running a little late. Could you meet me up at my hotel at about nine?"

She nodded. "That sounds fine."

Three

That same night, Clinton Ayers drew deeply on his long brown cigarette and let his gaze roam around his club. It had been of the utmost importance to him that the Ayers Club be the epitome of elegance and good taste. To that end, the decor had been painstakingly carried out to his exact specifications. The thick plush carpet was the precise shade of his favorite red Bordeaux that he kept stocked in his wine cellar. The red ebony that paneled the walls had been imported at great cost from Madagascar. The gaming tables were of the best mahogany, and the high-quality mechanisms of the roulette tables operated with barely a sound. Only the elite were admitted to his club.

The club was a far cry from the rat-infested hole in which he had been raised, and usually he got a deep sense of gratification from this fact. But nothing had been able to appease him since the Pearls of Sharah had been stolen from him.

His eyes met those of Caroline Jeffries. Her violet eyes sent him a secret look, then she returned her attention to the man beside her. She had been leaving messages with his secretary for days now. They had had a brief but extremely heated liaison a few weeks back, and Caroline obviously wanted a repeat performance. Perhaps, he thought idly. Perhaps.

He made his way through his club, nodding at this person and that, stopping occasionally to speak to those he considered amusing or useful. Spying Viscount Edward Willoughby at the roulette table, he paused for a moment, then made his way over to Tully. He was a large Scot who had a full head of shocking red hair. His special value to Clinton came from carrying out orders without question. "See to it that Willoughby loses tonight," Clinton told him.

With a nod Tully walked away, and Clinton, after grinding out his cigarette, moved on.

Lord Reginald St. Clair stood under a marble arch and watched Clinton Ayers. As usual, Clinton was dressed all in black, and his dark hair fell with an arrogant casualness to just above his shoulders. Reginald knew that women, both single and married, fought to gain Clinton's attention. Being as objective as possible, Reginald admitted that Clinton had a certain magnetism about him, plus a dark, brooding quality that women obviously found irresistible.

But Reginald knew that beneath the cultured and personable man Clinton presented to the world, there was an entirely different person. Turmoil and violence hid beneath his smooth exterior.

Clinton turned suddenly and saw St. Clair and the dislike written on his face. A smile curved Clinton's sensual lips, and he strolled across the room to the older man.

Reginald saw the smile for what it was: danger.

"Good evening, St. Clair. Gambling tonight?"

"Not here. You see, it's lately occurred to me that your club is the only place in town where I consistently lose."

"Nonsense. You've won here many times."

"At first," Reginald agreed.

Clinton shrugged nonchalantly. "At any rate, you've nearly taken care of your debt. You should give us another chance. Who knows? If you're lucky, maybe tonight you can put away the last part of that debt."

"Or maybe I'd find myself more in debt to you."

"I guess that's why it's called gambling." Clinton nodded to Amanda Radford, who had just come into the club. She was wearing a blue silk strapless evening gown whose bodice was so low, her full breasts appeared in danger of spilling out. She was obvious, but there were times when he was in the mood for the obvious, and tonight was one of those times. Maybe in her body he would find a little relief from the raw, open wound that had been left inside him by the disappearance of the pearls. He watched as she took a seat at a blackjack table and smiled up at the dealer, Nigel.

"Your message said you wanted to see me," Reginald said. "What is it?"

Clinton turned back to Reginald. "Yes. I was just wondering whether you'd heard. I had a priceless necklace stolen from the safe in my flat last week."

Reginald looked at the other man with shock. "Bloody hell. You must be devastated."

Clinton smiled thinly. "Quite. The theft was obviously done by a professional, someone with a deft touch and the knowledge of just what he wanted."

"Oh?" Reginald's face now expressed polite interest. "And what does Scotland Yard have to say?"

"As you well know, I can't contact them. However, I do have my organization working on the matter." Clinton drew out another cigarette and lit it. He pulled deeply on the cigarette, then exhaled, never once breaking eye contact with Reginald. "I'm going to get my pearls back one way or the other, St. Clair."

"I wish you all good luck, I'm sure. But why are you telling *me*?"

"Because I thought you should know . . . aristocratic blue blood spills as easily as common red blood. Have a nice evening, St. Clair."

In his hotel room Michael placed a call to Paris.

"I haven't learned anything from her, but my gut instinct tells me she's not involved." He listened. "I know—the pearls and her job. It does look suspicious, but I'm telling you, I don't think she has active knowledge of this case." He was silent for a moment, and his face tightened grimly. "The pearls may very well be the key, and I'll stay with her. I've already made arrangements to see her tomorrow night. In fact, she's picking me up here. Before that, though, I have a meeting with Nigel." He plowed his hands through the thickness of his hair. "Just stay near the phone. I'll keep in touch."

He slammed down the receiver, frustrated and angry. *Those damned pearls.* Why did Raine have them? And why did she seem so reluctant to talk about them?

Damn, he hoped his instinct about her not being involved was right, but it didn't look good for her. The industrial espionage ring had to have knowledge of what was being carried and when. Who better to give them that information than one of the couriers?

But not Raine, he thought. Please, God, not Raine.

He was very much afraid that his professionalism on this case had gone right out the window. He leaned back in the chair and rubbed his face tiredly. *What was he going to do if she was guilty?*

The next night Raine wore the pearls looped around her neck so that the gleaming rope fell in three layers down the front of her amethyst velvet gown.

The hotel desk manager looked with something like reverence at the stunningly lovely young woman in front of him. "Mr. Carr sent a message that he'll be down as soon as possible. I believe he had a meeting that ran late and he's just changing."

Raine's smile took the hotel manager's breath away as she pulled the long velvet stole that matched her gown more tightly around her. "It's a lovely night. I'll wait in the garden."

The moon was bright over Mayfair, and the small garden was charmingly lit by gaslight. Raine made her way along the path, deep in thought, clutching the velvet stole together at her throat. When a man stepped out of the shadows, she started and gave a small cry of fright.

Reginald put his hand on her arm. "Sorry, darling, it's only me."

"Father, what on earth are you doing here?"

"I saw you getting into a taxi outside your flat, but I couldn't catch your attention in time, so I hailed one of my own and followed you."

"But why?"

He threw a quick glance over his shoulder. "Just listen to me. I have very little time. I'm in a spot of trouble, and I have to leave the country for a time."

"Lord, Father, what's happened?"

"Now, darling, I don't want you to be alarmed.

I'm sure this will all blow over within a few months."

"Months? For heaven's sake, tell me what's wrong."

"No. I just wanted you to know that I'm going away, but while I'm gone you mustn't tell anyone that you've seen me or that I've left the country."

"Does that mean someone will be asking?"

"I hope not." He cast another furtive glance over his shoulder. "It was for this very reason that I've tried hard to keep our lives separate. Most of my associates don't realize you're my daughter."

"Father, you're frightening me."

He reached for her hand, unclenching it from the stole, and the amethyst velvet slowly slipped away from her neck. "I don't want you to be frightened, Raine, but—*what in God's name are you doing wearing that necklace?*"

"What?" Her hand went to her throat and the pearls and she gave a slightly embarrassed laugh. "I know you've always told me to keep the things you bring to my flat secreted away, and you've brought jewelry before. It's just that this one piece is so incredibly beautiful. There's something so special about it. I wore it the other night and told myself I wouldn't wear it again. But tonight . . . the dress just seemed to cry for the pearls. . . ." Her voice trailed off as the look of horror on her father's face registered.

Intensely urgent now, he took her shoulders in

his hands. "Raine, you must return to your flat immediately and put away that necklace!"

"I don't understand."

"That necklace is the reason I have to leave the country. Bloody hell. There's no time for me to explain. I must leave. But promise me, you'll take it back to your flat straightaway. No one must see it."

"All right, I will. But, Father, when will I see you again?"

"I don't know." His hold gentled on her. "I'm sorry, darling. I know I've confused and frightened you. Just remember that I love you very much, and I'll get in touch with you when I can." He pressed a tender kiss to her cheek and melted back into the shadows.

Michael stood in the hotel's doorway, frozen by the scene he had just witnessed in the garden. He had seen the furtive glances the man in the deep shadows had thrown repeatedly over his shoulder. Obviously, the man had felt it important to keep the meeting secret. Michael wished desperately he could have gotten a better look at the man . . . while he also fervently wished there might be an innocent explanation for the meeting.

Her hand absently fingering the pearls, Raine slowly turned and saw him. She forced a smile to her face and waited for him to come to her.

"I'm sorry I kept you waiting," he said, taking in the pallor of her skin.

"No, I'm the one who has to apologize. I'm going to have to cancel out this evening."

He almost swore aloud. "Does your canceling have anything to do with the man to whom you were just speaking?"

His question caught her off guard, and she panicked, uncertain how to answer him. But loyalty and concern for her father made her quickly recover, and she withdrew behind an aloof expression. "You're mistaken. I wasn't speaking with anyone."

Michael felt his stomach knot sickeningly. She had just looked at him with those fascinating rain-colored eyes of hers and lied to him. His mouth formed a grim line. "I was sure I saw someone with you."

Her gaze lowered away from him. "There was no one," she said firmly. "You must have seen a shadow."

A surge of anger shook him. He wanted to take her by the shoulder and demand to know why she was lying to him. But a stupid pride that had nothing to do with professionalism made him take a different tack. "All right, then. Why are you canceling our evening?"

"I—I've developed a headache while I was waiting, and I think it's best I go back to my flat."

"Then I'll take you," he said quietly.

"I'd really prefer that you didn't."

"I insist." With every appearance of solicitude, he put his arm around her, pulled her to his side, and began leading her back into the hotel. He felt the tremors in her body, tried not to care, and failed miserably.

• • •

Raine closed her bedroom door behind her, then stared at it, envisioning the man on the other side. Michael had refused to leave, saying he didn't like the idea of her being alone if she wasn't feeling well. Perhaps she should have used another excuse, although she had no idea what it could have been. She had told her fair amount of social white lies in her life, but lying to Michael was another matter. The lie had hurt her.

There had been a noticeable tension between them on the cab ride back to her flat. Or maybe all the tension had been on her part. Trying to deal with Michael's effect on her while worrying about her father was not conducive to tranquility. She was in a turmoil and didn't know what to do about either man.

She had known from the time she was a little girl that her father was not anyone's idea of a proper father. He was capricious and idiosyncratic. But he was also charming and very sweet. Even her mother, who freely admitted she married him for his title, had succumbed to his charms for a little while. He cheerfully went his own way in life, abiding by what he called his principles, and was a gentleman down to his immaculately kept fingernails.

Raine couldn't imagine what "spot of trouble" he could be in. The necklace, he had said, was the reason he had to leave the country.

She unclasped the pearls, unwound them from

around her neck, and held them in her cupped hands. The pearls gleamed with a luminescence unusual even in the best of pearls. But it was strange that she'd felt tempted to wear them; she rarely wore jewelry of any kind. She stared at them a moment longer, her brows drawn together, but the pearls offered her no answers, and finally she put them carefully away. Then she steeled herself to face the problem of Michael.

When she came back into the room, Michael put down the small enameled box he had been examining and turned to her, control evident in each of his movements. The first thing he noticed was that she no longer wore the pearl necklace. "You were gone so long, I was beginning to worry about you. Did you take something for your headache?"

"No. That is, I'm feeling somewhat better." His suit jacket lay over the back of a chair; his tie hung loose around his neck; the top buttons of his shirt were undone. She'd never seen him look more hard or more desirable. As far as her emotions went, her plan to proceed cautiously with Michael was not working.

"I'm glad to hear it. Would you like to go on to your friend's party, then?"

"No," she said abruptly.

He studied her. The soft color that normally blushed her cheeks remained absent, and the serenely cool composure that was so much a part of her was missing. Clearly, she was troubled about something. He thought of the man he had seen her speaking with in the hotel garden, and his anger grew. Enough was enough.

"Where are your pearls?"

"I put them away. And as I've told you before, they're not mine."

"Whoever gave them—"

"*Lent* them to me."

"—lent them to you must love you very much." He crossed his arms over his chest and seemed to give the matter grave thought. "I don't know any woman who could bear to part with such a treasure. So it must have been a man. Was it, Raine? Was it a man who lent them to you?"

"Why do you keep harping on this subject? It's just a pearl necklace. I want us to drop the subject."

"Oh, come on. You can't blame me for being curious."

Her nerves were on edge, and it showed in the sharpness of her voice. "You're *interrogating* me, Michael."

"Well, maybe I wouldn't have to if you told me what I want to know."

"Why should I? I don't really know you. Three days ago I didn't even know you existed."

"But you do now." His words dropped into the tension-filled air between them like pieces of hot lead.

She put a hand to her head and massaged her temple with her fingertips.

His eyes narrowed. "Is your headache worse?"

"No, but now that I'm home, I think I should make it an early night."

"You're asking me to leave?"

She nodded, then clenched her hands together so tightly, her knuckles turned white. "I hope you don't mind."

"Actually, I do mind." He slid his hands into the pockets of his trousers and closed the distance between them. "I mind a hell of a lot."

His nearness rattled her; her heart thudded painfully in her chest. "I know I've ruined our evening, and I apologize."

"I don't want your apologies, Raine. I want you to tell me what's wrong. I know you're upset about something."

"My headache—"

"Don't lie to me again."

If his voice had been raised, she might have continued the charade of the headache, but suddenly his tone had softened so that it sounded almost as if he were pleading. She didn't know what to say.

"Raine." He cupped his hand around her jaw and lifted her face so that she looked at him. "I know you were talking to a man in the garden. It was no shadow that I saw. Who was he?"

So he had known all along that she had lied to him. The knowledge made her feel worse. "Don't ask me. I can't tell you."

"Why, Raine? Who is he to you, and why are you protecting him?"

Confiding her personal troubles to other people

had always been hard for her. Maybe in Michael she had found someone— She stopped herself. What did she really know about him? He was an American in London on business. He had a mother in Albuquerque who sent him chocolate chip cookies. And she was falling in love with him.

Lord, she felt torn. But her father rarely asked anything of her, and she felt she had to honor his request that she not tell anyone she had seen him or that he had left the country. Hopefully, her father had exaggerated the trouble he was in, but until she knew more, she couldn't—wouldn't! —betray his confidence.

Michael's frustration grew as Raine's silence continued. "For God's sake, Raine, if you're in trouble, let me help you."

"I'm not in any trouble."

She pulled her face from his grasp and tried to move away from him, but he wrapped his long fingers around her upper arms, stopping her. "Don't walk away from me. Look at me. Talk to me."

He genuinely cared. She could hear it in his voice, and her heart turned over. How was she going to resist him now? "Michael, please don't worry about me."

"But I do." His voice was low, urgent, rough. "Dammit, Raine, you're making me absolutely crazy. What are you up to?"

"Nothing." She searched her mind for a way to appease him and make him drop the subject. "The

fact that I can't tell you who I was talking to shouldn't affect us. The . . . the person in the garden has nothing to do with you and me."

"Doesn't he? You lied to me about him."

She put her hands on his chest, unconsciously wanting to soothe him, wanting to soften his hard expression. "I'm sorry about that. I don't like to lie, but in this case I felt it was necessary."

He knew all about lies being necessary, and he'd be a hypocrite if he continued to harangue her about the lie. He hated the deceit between them. Hers. His. *Dammit.* He felt boxed in. Training and job versus caring for her and wanting her almost beyond endurance. It should have been more of a contest, but with her so near . . .

He put his arms around her waist. The velvet of her dress was gratifyingly sensual to the touch of his fingertips. "I don't want any secrets between us," he said, a basic, primitive possessiveness surfacing in his voice. Her erotic scent was invading his senses, making him forget the guilt he felt that the secrets weren't all on her side.

Her hands slid up to the faintly raspy skin of his face. "Don't think about it," she whispered, and touched his mouth with hers.

Fire crawled slowly through his veins. "Are you trying to seduce me?" he asked roughly.

"Yes," she said, surprised at herself. Before Michael, she would never have considered making advances to a man. Philip would have been appalled, and in truth, no other man had inspired such wanton behavior. She wanted to make Michael forget seeing her father in the hotel garden, but she also desperately wanted to have him make love to her. Faint tremors ran through Michael's arms as he held her, and she was thrilled and amazed that he was as affected by her as she was by him. "Can I seduce you?"

He pulled her harder against him, adjusting his height so that his pelvis fit tightly against hers. She was trying to give him something to think about other than the clandestine meeting in the garden, he thought, and she was succeeding beautifully. Dark anger vied with bright desire. "You can try," he muttered, and skimmed his lips down her throat.

She threw her head back and arched her neck. There was a tantalizing enjoyment in flirting with him, she discovered. This teasing prelude to love-making was like dancing through flames. Only there was no pain, just sweet heat. "How hard would I have to try?" she whispered.

"Not very damn hard at all. That's the hell of it." He brought his mouth back to hers and bit her lower lip with a barely controlled violence.

An intense, aching hunger was building in the pit of her stomach. She'd spent the past six years repressing all feelings of the heart and body. Now passion and love burst free. She thrust her tongue deep into his mouth and gave herself up to him.

He groaned and crushed her against him, kissing her long and hard. Then, in the next instant, he swept her up into his arms and headed for her bedroom.

He tore his mouth from hers long enough to open the door. He placed her on the lace-covered bed and came down beside her. They still had their clothes on, but it seemed almost beyond his ability to take the time to undress them. He felt as if his mouth had to be kissing her, his hands touching her, his body pressing against hers, or he would surely come apart.

"You're mine," he said, his mouth searing the skin of her neck.

"Yes."

He heard the sound of helplessness in her answer. "Lord, you drive me crazy," he muttered, and was grimly aware of the truth of what he said. He had never before put his personal needs ahead of his professional obligations, but . . . He skimmed open the zipper of her velvet gown and reached blindly for her breasts. "You feel like heaven in my hands," he said harshly. "What will you taste like?"

She inhaled a deep, jerky breath. "Michael, what are we doing to each other?" she asked, a hazy kind of wonder in her voice.

"I'll be damned if I know." He took her into his mouth, sucking the sweet, stiff peak. Reason was rapidly deserting him, but her question stayed with him in a small, cold, clear corner of his mind. She had admitted that she was trying to seduce him, and she had him burning for her. He wanted nothing more than to lose himself in her soft womanly depths and ease the need that clawed at him.

But her reason for seducing him galled him. When they made love, he wanted it to be clear there wasn't a single ulterior motive. Slowly, he pulled away from her, and an agony such as he'd never known racked him.

She opened her eyes, and her gaze revealed her complete lack of comprehension at why he had drawn away from her. She knew only that her breasts were swollen and aching from his caresses, and that her lips were reddened and alive from his deep, forceful kisses. She reached for him.

He moved abruptly away. "Don't!"

She ran her tongue over her tingling bottom lip. "I don't understand," she whispered. "What's wrong?"

He attempted to straighten the amethyst velvet dress that was twisted around her, but he kept brushing her bare skin, and his hand was irritatingly unsteady. "I've got to get out of here." He rolled off the bed and to his feet.

"Michael?"

She was so beautiful, he thought. Her porcelain-fine skin showed marks of his lovemaking, and her usually neatly coiffed hair lay in shining disarray around her head. Because he wanted so badly to go back to her, his voice was exceptionally gruff. "Tomorrow. We'll talk tomorrow."

He turned on his heel and strode out.

Raine closed her eyes, rolled over, and buried her face in the pillow. For the first time in six years she had opened herself up to a man—*a man with whom she had fallen quickly but earnestly in love*—and he had rebuffed her.

How had her life gotten in such a state in just three short days, she asked herself.

And then the tears began to flow.

Four

Raine loved her mother and her father, and she had loved Philip. But each of these people in different ways had taught her the same hard lesson: the safest way to get through life was to detach oneself emotionally from others. Raine had learned that she could depend only on herself. Now Michael had added to her education. And so, after a near sleepless night, Raine gathered herself together, retreated behind a wall of cool reserve, and went to work.

When she walked into Cameron's office, Edward was there, sunglasses hiding what she was sure were bloodshot eyes. She nodded to Cameron, then directed her gaze to her friend. "Good morning. It's lovely to see you, but your presence this early can mean only that you haven't been to bed yet."

Edward lowered his dark glasses and peered

over their rims at her. "You don't look any too well rested yourself."

She thought of the night just past, the tears she had shed, and the hours she'd spent tossing and turning. "You're mistaken."

The frosty look she gave him had no effect on him. "Good. I'm glad to hear it. Then the dark circles under your eyes must be just smudged mascara."

Concern for her appearance made her automatically rub a finger beneath her eyes. Edward grinned.

"If you two are quite finished," Cameron interjected, "I do have business to conduct."

"I was wondering what I was doing here this early," Edward drawled.

Raine sank into a chair beside him and bit her tongue to keep herself from making a sarcastic comment. It wasn't like her to snipe at Edward. She must be more tired than she realized. *Tired and hurt.* But, she vowed, she'd get over Michael just as she had gotten over all the other hurts in her life.

"Raine, Mr. Birtwilder has requested you again," Cameron said.

"Potty old bird," Edward muttered.

Raine jumped to defend the elderly gentleman she'd come to know over the last year through numerous courier trips to his home. "Horace may be eccentric, but he's *very* nice."

"But potty, right? I mean, what else would you

call him, living as he does as a virtual recluse in that mausoleum in Switzerland."

"He has his art and his work there. He's very contented. Unlike some people, he doesn't feel the need for a frenetic lifestyle. He had it once; he doesn't want it now."

"His collection of art impresses me," Edward said, "but his work doesn't. He putters about a laboratory and fancies himself an inventor, but as far as I can see, nothing he's come up with is of any import or practicality at all."

Cameron was patiently studying the end of his pencil. "I guess that attitude explains why the old gentleman began requesting Raine. She takes on over his latest design."

Raine expected another caustic rejoinder from Edward. Instead, he took off his dark glasses and looked at her, and just for a moment Raine thought she caught a glimpse of something other than ennui in his eyes.

"At least there's no danger that you'll be bopped over the head for his papers," he said. "He's never had us carry anything in the least significant. I think he employs a courier service just to make himself feel important."

"It's little enough, Edward," she said mildly. "He pays the fee, and I don't mind flying over and staying the night. His mausoleum, as you call his house, is fascinating, and I always feel as if my visits make him happy." And right about now, a trip out of the country might do her good, she thought wearily.

"Raine, a man would have to be dead not to be happy having you at the other end of a dinner table to look at."

Cameron tossed his pencil down. "Right, so that's settled then. Raine, my secretary has your ticket. I calculate you have plenty of time to run by the office of Birtwilder's solicitor to fetch the packet, drop by your flat, pack a bag, then make Heathrow."

Raine stood, but after hesitating she turned to Edward. "Do you have an assignment this morning?"

He nodded. "Two actually."

"You will be careful, won't you?"

He came to his feet. "There's nothing to worry about. There hasn't been a theft in a couple of weeks now. Besides, I have an exceptionally hard head."

"I've noticed," she said dryly. "Nevertheless, I would hate to see it dented."

He grinned. "That makes two of us."

Outside Cameron's office, his secretary handed Raine the tickets. "There's someone waiting for you in the outer office."

She glanced at the tickets, then slipped them into her purse. "Oh?"

"I told him you were in a meeting, but he insisted on waiting." The young woman's voice switched from a business tone to one heavy with meaning. "A Yank. A very *interesting*-looking Yank."

Raine tensed. Michael, of course. The hurt of his rejection lay just beneath the surface, and any defenses against him she had managed to conjure up during the night now felt extremely fragile. She didn't want to face him, but she seemed to have no choice. Besides, she asked herself, what could he do to her that he hadn't already done? He wouldn't reject her again, because she wouldn't give him the opportunity.

With a newfound strength she squared her shoulders and headed for the outer office. A faint hope that he had given up the wait and left was dashed as soon as she opened the door.

The room was empty except for Michael, and at the sound of her entry he thrust aside the magazine through which he had been leafing and stood.

He was dressed in a dark blue suit that had been tailored to perfectly fit his broad shoulders and large frame. He had such a forceful presence, he seemed to fill the entire room, and she felt some of her newfound strength ebb away.

"We need to talk, Raine."

"I don't have time." As if to prove her point, she glanced at her watch. "I have a flight to catch."

His expression sharpened. "Where are you going?"

"Switzerland. Now, if you'll excuse me . . ." She started to walk past him, but he stepped in front of her, blocking her path.

In the lonely hours of the night his anger had vanished, leaving only his obsession for her. "Raine—"

"I have nothing to say to you, Michael."

He uttered a mild expletive. "That's the whole problem, isn't it? You won't confide in me."

She wrapped her arms around her waist, her posture stiff. Her throat felt tight, but she forced a calm, detached, polite tone into her words. "I was sure we had covered this subject last night. Since you've brought it up again, however, I'll concede that you're right: I won't confide in you. Now, is that all? Because if it is, I must leave now."

He took her by the arms. "Dammit, Raine, I *had* to walk out last night. I wanted you like hell. I still want you. But when we make love, I want to make sure it's not because you're trying to get my mind off some other man."

Pain and bewilderment rushed into her gray eyes. "But I wanted you."

"I believe you," he said, his voice rough and fierce, his hold tightening on her arms. "Up to a point. The kind of heat you were throwing off can be faked only so far, and then the real thing has got to take over."

Raine flushed as she remembered her abandon. Even now, a betraying need was seeping through her.

"But it's the *reason* behind all of that wild seductiveness that throws up a red light for me. I've already figured out that the man in the garden must mean a hell of a lot to you—so much to you in fact that you were willing to go to bed with me to distract my attention from him. But I have to ask one thing. Does he know of this great sacrifice you were so eager to make for him?"

Her face lost all color. "Stop it," she whispered. "Just stop it."

He watched her turn white, heard the pain in her voice, and felt himself go soft inside. Dammit, she was getting to him. Of its own accord, his tone gentled. "Raine, you're involved in something that's dangerous, not to mention illegal. Let me help you."

"What are you talking about?" she asked, bewildered. "If you think my meeting that man in your hotel garden was for illegal purposes, you're very wrong."

He studied her for a moment, then gave a heavy sigh. "You're not giving me many options, Raine."

"I still have no idea what you're talking about."

"I guess I'm going to have to play things your way. All right, then, you and I are going to go back to square one."

Raine felt as if she'd come late to the theater and missed the entire first act. "Michael, will you make sense?"

"There's only one thing that makes any sense between you and me, and that's this." Taking her completely by surprise, he pressed a hard kiss to her lips. Drawing back a little, he muttered, "How long will you be gone?"

"Just overnight."

"What time will you be back?"

"My flight arrives at three o'clock tomorrow afternoon at Heathrow."

His eyes were fixed on her mouth. "I'll be there to meet you. Don't make any plans."

Her heart was beating fast. "Why?"

His hands began to caress her arms. "We're going to pretend last night never happened. We're going to slow down, date, get to know each other better. Tomorrow evening we'll go to dinner. Perhaps take in a movie afterward. Open your mouth, Raine."

Involuntarily, her lips parted. She made a small indistinct sound, and he drew her against him and crushed his mouth to hers.

Late that night, in Horace Birtwilder's villa, Raine could still feel the effect of Michael's kiss. And she could hardly think of anything but him. He had given her new hope by saying that he wanted to start over in their relationship. She prayed she wasn't being a fool.

From the first he had thrown her into a turmoil, and things had progressed fast between them. He hadn't allowed her to withdraw from him as she usually did with men. He elicited passion in all forms from her. Whether they could slow things down between them remained to be seen. But she felt happy and excited, perhaps because this time, with this man, she wouldn't have to repress her love.

She wandered through the long, wide halls of the villa, stopping now and then to admire a work of art. Horace Birtwilder had been one of England's leading industrialists until, when he was fifty years old, his wife had died suddenly. Devastated, he had sold everything and retreated to Switzerland. For the past twenty years he had indulged himself in his two great passions—collecting art and working in his high-tech laboratory. His work rarely produced anything of interest to the outside world, but he was a satisfied man, and as far as Raine was concerned, that was what was important.

She stopped before a Cézanne and studied the subtle use of greens and golds in the exquisite painting of the Provençal landscape. After a few minutes she moved on. She should go to bed, she told herself. But even though it had been a long day and she hadn't gotten much rest the night before, she didn't feel ready to fall asleep. On impulse she headed for the library. Reading herself to sleep was an old trick, but one that always worked.

The library was a big, comfortable, well-used room, and one of her favorite places in the villa. Her hand closed over the knob, but a faint noise from within the room made her hesitate. Perhaps Horace had needed a book, she thought, but she could see no light from under the door. Curious, she opened the door and was greeted by darkness. Then her eyes were drawn across the room to an open window. Against the paler shade of the night, a dark form was outlined.

Quickly, she pressed the switch, flooding light into the room and onto the man dressed all in black who was straddling the windowsill.

Lord Reginald St. Clair.

"Father!"

Reginald blinked his eyes against the light and then focused with horror on his daughter. After a moment the tension went out of his body. "Good God, Raine, you scared me to death."

"*I* scared *you!* Father, what are you doing here? Why are you dressed like that? And *why* are you going out the window?" She pressed a hand to her forehead as a sudden thought struck her. "Lord, it's a second-story window!"

He gave her a distinctly sheepish grin and edged back into the room. "Do you think you might lower your voice, darling? We don't want to disturb Mr. Birtwilder, now, do we?"

She took in the utility belt around his waist and his black cap, turtleneck sweater, and slacks. "I think I'd better sit down," she muttered, and sank into a nearby chair.

He looked at her anxiously. "You're not going to be sticky about this, are you?"

Her gaze fixed on the long leather cylinder strapped to his back, then quickly scanned the room, stopping at a picture frame that had held a Picasso. The picture frame was empty. "Father, what have you done?"

"It was only a *little* Picasso, darling." With his black-gloved thumb and forefinger a scant centimeter apart, he showed her his idea of little. "And heaven knows, Birtwilder can certainly afford the loss."

"You're a thief," she said, her voice dull with shock.

He pulled at his ear. "I suppose that's one way of looking at the matter. But I want you to understand that my activities are entirely honorable."

"Honorable!"

"Shhh! Darling, do let us speak in whispers," he urged, and gave her a charming grin.

She rubbed her forehead as certain things began clicking into place. The art objects he had brought to her flat for "safekeeping." And the *pearls.* She supposed she had been incredibly stupid.

"It's really been an unexpected bonus seeing you tonight," her father said, hovering between her and the window, "but, upon reflection, I think the best thing for me to do is to be on my way now."

She came out of her chair and advanced on him until they were standing toe to toe. "You're going to stay right where you are until you explain everything to me, including why you think it's honorable to stash your stolen art objects in *my* flat."

His expression turned serious. "I suppose it was inevitable that you would figure that one out. You're very bright taking after my side of the family like you do."

"Father," she said threateningly.

"You've never been in any danger, Raine. I've seen to that."

"By keeping our lives separate, you mean? It wouldn't take a deep search into Debrett's *Peerage* to find out that we're father and daughter."

"The people about whom I'm concerned have never heard of Debrett's *Peerage*."

She regarded him steadily. "All right. Perhaps leading separate lives has kept me safe from your more unsavory associates"—words momentarily failed her when she tried to imagine her fastidious father associating with members of the underworld—"but what if you were caught and Scotland Yard came to search my flat? I would be an accessory."

"Darling, that would never happen. I am, quite simply, the *best*. Why, do you know the chaps at Scotland Yard and Interpol have taken to calling me 'the Ghost'?"

She stared at him in disbelief.

"I know. I don't entirely understand it myself. It's a bit fanciful, if you ask me." He cast an uneasy eye toward the door and put a hand on her arm. "I realize what a shock this is to you, but I really do think I should be pushing off now. Meet me tomorrow night, and I will explain everything."

Her eyes narrowed suspiciously.

"I promise, darling. I won't stand you up. I changed my mind about leaving, and I'm still in London. You know how I've never been able to take the Continent for long periods of time. I just slip over every now and then for the odd job here and there. At any rate, I took a room in the Elephant and Castle area." He made a face. "No one who knows me will expect to find me there. Needless to say, I'm not happy with my new residence, but I'm hopeful I can return to St. James soon."

"Where do you want me to meet you?" she asked, her jaw clenched so tightly, it hurt.

"There's a coffee house near the tube stop. Rather an artsy spot. Stays open 'til the wee hours. You can't miss it. I'll be there at midnight." He dropped a kiss on her cheek and started for the open window.

"Father."

He looked back at her.

She held out her hand. "I'll have the Picasso."

"But—"

"Give it to me."

With great reluctance he reached behind him, unscrewed the lid of the cylinder, withdrew the rolled-up painting, and handed it to her. "What are you going to do?"

"I'll just have to tell Horace that I surprised a burglar going out the window, and he dropped this. You didn't leave anything behind, did you?"

He gave a loud sigh. "Darling, I am a professional. I don't make mistakes." At the window he gave her a jaunty salute, then climbed out.

She rushed forward and peered out, just in time to see her father skimming nimbly down a vine-covered drainpipe. "Be careful," she whispered.

Reginald reached the ground, sent a beaming, adoring smile up to her, then disappeared into the darkness.

Raine stepped back from the window, shaken. If she had had a dream in which she had caught her father climbing out a window with a Picasso strapped to his back, she would have laughed it off as totally impossible. But the painting in her hand was proof that the last few minutes had not been a dream. And now she had to face the very nice owner of the painting, lie to him, and somehow be convincing.

When Raine's plane landed at Heathrow the next afternoon, she felt surprisingly rested. Horace had accepted her story without question and been embarrassingly grateful.

It had been a surprise to Raine when he had decided not to notify the authorities of the break-in, but she supposed from his point of view the decision made sense. Thanks to Raine, he said, nothing had been taken, and he certainly didn't want to alert his insurance company. They would most assuredly raise his premium. They'd been after him for some time to install an adequate alarm system. But, he told her, he was working on a system of his own, and he wouldn't be hurried.

Then he had his housekeeper put Raine to bed with a warm glass of milk, as if she were a little girl who had undergone a terrible trauma. He wasn't far wrong, but his decision not to call the authorities had eased her mind considerably, and she had fallen instantly asleep.

Now, after clearing customs, she looked around for Michael. When she saw no sign of him, she experienced a stab of disappointment. It frightened her to realize how much she had been looking forward to seeing him, as if by going into his arms she would find a safe, dependable haven in a world that seemed determined not to give her anything to hold on to. It was a foolish way for her to think.

She walked outside into a fine rainfall. And then she saw Michael, standing by a dark blue Aston-Martin, smiling at her. Her heart lightened, and she walked to his side.

"Hi," he said softly, taking her bag. "Did you have a nice trip?"

She nodded. "When I didn't see you inside, I thought you'd forgotten."

His eyes darkened. "How could I forget? I've been counting the hours."

"I have too," she confessed, the need for caution slipping out of her mind.

He opened the door for her, and she climbed in. He deposited her suitcase in the backseat, then walked around and slid in beside her.

"Is this your car?"

"It's mine while I'm in England. Are you hungry?"

"No." She tried not to stare at him, but he was filling up her senses. The big, tough look of him, the nearness and warmth of him, and the heady scent of him assaulted her with a massive dose of sensuality.

He smiled at her. "Then why don't we drop your bag off at your flat, let you freshen up, and then decide how we're going to spend the rest of the day and evening."

"All right."

His smile broadened. "Tell me about your trip,"

he said, directing the car out into the stream of traffic.

"It was just a routine delivery," she said, wondering how she had become so adept at lying. But the extraordinary revelation that her father was a cat burglar was not something she was ready to share with anyone. First she wanted to hear her father's story, which she would do later on. Then she would decide what to do. "By the way, whatever we do, I'd like to get home early."

"Oh?" He reached for her hand. "Did the trip tire you out?"

"Traveling is always tiring, isn't it?"

She hadn't answered his question directly, he realized, but then, his question had been an idle one. At a stoplight, he leaned toward her. "I'm really happy that you consented to see me tonight," he whispered, his mouth almost brushing her cheek.

"If I hadn't, you would have kept trying, wouldn't you?"

He nodded. "You're getting to know me well. Maybe time isn't all it's cracked up to be."

She stared deep into his eyes, saw the desire simmering there, and found she could barely speak. "What do you do to me? I don't understand."

"Maybe understanding isn't all that important either." He was still whispering, and this time he did allow his lips to touch her cheek. "It's so damn good to be this close to you."

She took a deep breath and raised her hand to his head. "You have raindrops in your hair."

"London rain. London fog. London sunshine. I've been with you in all three."

"Which do you like the best?"

He was studying her lips. "Wait until we make love in all three and I'll let you know."

"You said—"

A horn honked behind them, and he started the car forward.

"I know. I said we'd start from square one. Go slow." He glanced at her. "Do you think it's possible?"

"I don't know."

"I'm going to try, Raine. Heaven knows, I will. But I take one look at you, and I want to crawl all over you."

She tore her gaze away from him and stared out the rain-spattered window, willing the heat inside her to die down. She wouldn't want him so much once they were out of the close confines of the car, she told herself. When they pulled up in front of her flat, she breathed a sigh of relief.

Five

Michael placed Raine's bag on the floor of her bedroom and started back toward the sitting room, fully intending to enjoy the afternoon and evening ahead without attempting to elicit information from her. It was a very unprofessional attitude for him to take. But there was something extremely real, solid, and perfect between the two of them, and he was sure that when she was ready, she would confide in him.

Somehow she was involved in the industrial espionage organization, but his instincts were telling him her involvement was innocent. He wasn't sure how this could be possible, but he stubbornly clung to his belief.

Professionally, he would keep his eyes and ears open; personally, he would protect her at all costs. He had other leads he was working on. Sooner or later he would break the theft ring. And in the meantime, if headquarters didn't like it, they could take a flying leap off the Eiffel Tower.

"Would you like some tea?" Raine asked as he walked into the room.

The urge to touch her was too great to repress. He went to her and took her in his arms. "I guess what I'd like and what I'll get are two different things. Lord, you're so beautiful."

Her lips curved into a rueful grin, and she stepped away. "And you're impossible. I thought you were going to try."

"I *am* trying. It's just that you're too damned desirable."

She stilled, staring at him with wonderment. "No one's ever told me that before—not in that way. Men have wanted me before, but it's always been a highly civilized kind of wanting. Your desire for me is raw and powerful."

Her soft words coiled through him, a river of fire burning his insides. He shot a desperate look at the ceiling. "Do you have a newspaper? We'd better decide fast what we're going to do this evening, and get the hell out of here."

His need was there for her to see, naked and potent, and it left Raine shaken. The control over her own feelings was quickly dissolving beneath an onslaught of heat. Her teeth fastened on her bottom lip, and she glanced vaguely around. "Yesterday's paper should be around here somewhere."

"Get it," he said roughly, and in the next breath asked, "If my desire for you is raw and powerful, what is your desire for me like? *How* do you want me, Raine? *Do* you want me?"

She gave one nod in answer to all of his questions. "I'll get the paper."

He grabbed her arm as she went to move past him. "Are you *certain* you want me, or do you have a motive for telling me that?"

"I'm being as honest with you as I know how, Michael."

"How I want to believe you." He dropped her arm and threaded his fingers through her hair so that his hands were cupping either side of her head and exerting pressure. "Do you have another man in this beautiful head of yours, Raine? Because if you do . . ."

She wasn't sure her knees would support her much longer. She felt weak and hot. "I don't," she whispered. "How could I? You're like that fog we first met in. You're overwhelming, all-encompassing. Without even touching me you wrap me up and obscure my vision, preventing me from seeing anyone but you. And when you touch me . . ."

Easing the pressure, his fingertips gently caressed her scalp. But his voice stayed harsh and rough. "What, Raine? When I touch you, what?"

She gazed up at him helplessly. "I go up in flames."

He groaned and began pushing her backward. "I tried, Lord knows I did. I thought I could be with you without having you. But I was wrong. My need for you overrides everything, even my common sense. I'm sorry." When her back hit the wall, he pressed his hard body down on hers and crushed his mouth to her lips.

Raine couldn't think of a single reason to fight against the blazing passion between them. All her life she had wanted a man to love, a strong man to whom she could cling and on whom she could depend, a man who would hold her tight, desire and love her, and never let her go. Michael was that man.

His big hand fumbled with the buttons of her blouse, grew impatient, and pulled at the fabric. The silk gave, and his hand delved into her bra to close around her breast. "You're so full and soft," he whispered hoarsely. "Why do you have so many clothes on?"

"They'll come off." She reached between their bodies to pull apart the edges of her blouse, then worked out of it and started unbuttoning his shirt.

He pushed the straps of her bra off her shoulders and took hold of both breasts, kneading and caressing, and all the while hungrily kissing her. Frustration ate at him; fever swamped him. He thrust his pelvis against her, and her softness nearly undid him. "This isn't going to work," he groaned, and swept her into his arms. "I want you on a bed, under me."

She wrapped her arms tightly around his neck and pressed her mouth to the strong column of his throat. When he reached the side of the bed, he lowered her to the floor, and within minutes their clothes were spread around their feet.

"We should go slow," he said, his eyes hungrily consuming her.

She moved against him, wantonly pressing her breasts into his hair-roughened chest. "I don't want it slow." She angled her head and spread kisses over his chest. "I've waited all my life to make love to you. I can't be patient." She closed her mouth over one of his nipples, licked, then lightly bit.

He jerked violently, then took her down with him onto the bed, with him on top of her. "You'd better stop talking that way," he said, his voice vibrating with intense feeling, "or I'll be inside you so fast you won't know what hit you."

"Do it." She raked her nails down his spine and felt muscles and smooth skin.

A shudder racked his powerful body. "Raine!" In agony he raised up, and in one smooth, fast push, entered her. She wrapped her legs around his body, accepting all of him instantly.

Fire rushed to his brain, obliterating thought and the need to go slow this first time. Maddened, he moved in and out of her, savoring the exquisite tight feel of her. Distantly, he heard her say, "I love you," but his mind couldn't hold on to the words. His body was a mass of shattered nerve endings. Insanity lay just around the corner. He drove deep into her and heard her cry of pleasure.

How could anything be this good, he wondered dimly, and felt her nails bite into his back. His mouth ground down onto hers, and his tongue frantically coiled with hers. His rhythm quick-

ened, and she matched his pace, clutching at
him. Unable to take any more, he gripped her hips,
locking her to him, then everything started to
explode around them.

A long time later Michael awakened. Raine lay
in his arms, her legs entwined with his. He turned
his head on the pillow and heard rain pattering
against the window. Trying his best not to disturb her, he reached for the cover at the end of
the bed and drew it over them.

Without opening her eyes, Raine smiled. "I wasn't
cold; you keep me warm. When I met you in the
fog, I had the odd urge to use your warmth and
strength as I might a downy quilt and pull you
around me."

He shifted, gathered her fully into his arms,
and, without warning, slid into her. Looking down
into her rain-colored eyes, he asked, "How does it
feel to have me wrapped around you and in you?"

She drew a ragged breath. "Like fire. Like I'm
filled up with you. I don't know . . . I can't de-
scribe it. You're so big and hard and strong."

He made a slight movement of his hips. "I woke
up wanting you. I'll die wanting you."

She closed her eyes on a gasp. "Do that again."

"What? This?" He thrust, reaching deep and
high inside her, but just once.

"Oh, Michael . . . again."

He complied, once, twice, then stopped, and
kissed her softly. "I was made to fit inside you."

She opened her eyes. "I never want to be without you."

Something savage exploded in his brain, and he drove into her.

Raine came up out of the tube station at Elephant and Castle and glanced at her watch. Five minutes to midnight. She pushed her umbrella open against the rain, tucked her hand into a pocket of her trench coat, and began walking. Michael had been sleeping soundly when she left. She had hated leaving him, but she couldn't afford to miss this appointment with her father, because she had no idea how to get in touch with him any other way.

She located the coffee house halfway up the street. From the outside the old building appeared unpretentious. Inside, it boasted the artsy atmosphere her father had mentioned, and even at this time of night was about half full. Her father was sitting on a bench, his back to the wall, a table in front of him. She took a chair across from him.

He gave her a loving smile. "Hello, darling. How did things go last night after I left?"

For a moment her mind went blank. Had it been only last night that she had seen her father in Switzerland? The hours she had just spent making love with Michael had distorted time for her and changed her whole life. Yet the fact remained: her father, Lord Reginald St. Clair, was a cat burglar.

"You were lucky. Horace decided it would be best not to notify the authorities."

Reginald sat back, a satisfied expression on his face. "I knew it. Those insurance fellows have been pressing him hard to install an alarm system."

She looked at him with surprise. "How did you know that?"

"I told you—"

She held up her hand. "I know. You're the best."

He nodded. "Right. And between you and me, an alarm system wouldn't have deterred me one whit. Would you like a coffee, darling? I can recommend the espresso, or if you'd prefer something else?"

She folded her arms and rested them on the table. "All I want is answers."

"I suppose I should start at the beginning."

"Absolutely, and don't leave a thing out."

"Raine, I really see no reason why you should be so grim about the matter."

"Chalk it up to a flaw in my character, Father, and get on with it."

"Whatever you say, darling. Well, let's see, as you are aware, I've earned my living for many years by gambling. And that's true as far as it goes. It's just that some years ago I realized I needed a way to supplement my income, and I cast about in my mind for an occupation which I might enjoy and at which I would excel. Art came immediately to mind. You know what a connoisseur I am. Actually, art would have been my major at Cambridge if I hadn't been sent down the first year for—" He glanced at her, then quickly shook his head. "It's not really important. As I was saying, I faced the problem of how I could use this expert knowledge of mine so that it would be both lucrative and honorable."

"Honorable?"

"Raine, you must understand, I maintain only the highest of moral standards in my work. I steal only from people who can afford the loss, and I steal only small things"—he gave a nonchalant wave of his hand—"such as an insignificant Monet, for instance."

"Father, there is no such thing as an insignificant Monet."

"Of course there is. It's all a matter of perspective. At any rate, things were going swimmingly. Then I happened into the Ayers Club." He frowned. "Have you heard of it?"

"I've heard the name," she said slowly. "I think Edward has mentioned the club."

He grimaced. "Yes, well, when I started going there, I won with a regularity that was quite pleasing. But my winning streak soon ended. At first my losses were minimal, but then the losses began happening with more and more consistency and in bigger and bigger amounts until I was in tremendous debt."

"I don't believe this, Father. You've always been so good at gaming."

"Yes, well, as it turns out, I wasn't in control of the situation. The owner, Clinton Ayers, a blackguard of the first water, had somehow found out about my part-time occupation, and he saw a chance to add cheaply to his own art collection. He arranged for me to have an extraordinary run of bad luck at the tables, then blackmailed me into stealing for him."

"Oh, my Lord."

Reginald's face hardened with anger. "Quite. Stealing for the man went against all of my principles. Plus, I realized that the blackmail was an open-ended proposition that could possibly go on forever. So I devised a plan. As it happened, I knew that Ayers possessed a pearl necklace which he greatly prized." He gave a shrug. "So I stole the necklace."

"But why?"

"There were several things in my mind. Ultimately, I hoped I might use the pearls to negotiate my markers from him. Unfortunately, I badly underestimated his reaction. At first he had his people turn this town upside down. Then, after a few days, his attention focused on me. But not in the way that I had expected. He called me to the club, where he delivered a veiled threat. That same night I returned to my flat to find that it had been torn apart."

"I'm sorry about that, Father, but I don't know what you imagined would happen. After all, you did steal from the man."

"You don't understand. His threat didn't bother me. Neither did the fact that he had his thugs go through my flat. I had expected that."

"So what didn't you expect?"

"These thugs left a message for me in a particularly chilling fashion. Raine, do you remember the family portrait that was done when I was a child and that hangs over my fireplace?"

"Of course I do."

"That night I found 'twenty-four hours' scrawled across the portrait in blood."

"Blood?"

"Yes, and that's not all. In the painting my eyes had been gouged out."

"Father!"

He reached over and grasped her hand. "Please don't be distressed. Everything's going to be all right. Now that I understand the full extent of the danger I'm dealing with, I plan to lay low for a while until Ayers's temper cools. Then I'll negotiate with him."

"Do you honestly think he can be dealt with?"

Reginald opened his mouth to speak, shut it, then gave a heavy sigh. "No."

Worried, Raine studied her father. All of her life this man had been her champion and her hero, and she loved him very much. It wasn't hard for her to come to a decision.

"All right," she said. "For obvious reasons we can't go to the authorities. And you can't go running about. So I'm going to help you."

Stern, he held up a finger. "Absolutely not. You will *not* become involved."

"What are you talking about? I'm *already* involved. Have you forgotten the pearls you brought to me to keep for you? Clinton Ayers's pearls, as a matter of fact. The ones he's obviously ready to kill to get back."

"I've made a lot of mistakes, Raine, but I will not compound my bad judgment by getting you further involved in this. We will meet here again tomorrow night, and you will give me back everything you are currently holding for me."

She sat back, crossed her arms over her chest, and stared fixedly at him.

"Don't look at me like that. I have no intention of permitting you to put yourself in danger for me. I've lived this double life for a long time, and I've always managed. Things will turn right eventually."

"Have you ever come up against anyone like Clinton Ayers before?"

"No, I haven't, but—"

"Look, I'm not exactly sure yet what I can do, but I swear I'll be careful. I just want your promise that you'll keep out of sight and give up your midnight forays into houses that are not your own."

"Darling—"

"Promise me."

He threw up his hands. "That stubbornness must come from your mother's side of the family. I can't change your mind, can I?"

"No, you can't."

"All right, then, but you must keep in constant touch with me. I want to know what you are doing, and I must be assured that you'll be safe. I'm not at all easy about this."

All of Raine's life her father had given her the impression that he was undefeatable. Now, a barely discernible slumping of his shoulders and a slight lessening of the twinkle in his eye betrayed to Raine his feeling of being old and tired for the first time in his life.

She reached across the table and took his hand. "Everything will be all right."

Michael awoke to find that he was alone in bed. He sat up, puzzled and annoyed and feeling a peculiar desolation because Raine wasn't in his arms. A glance at the bedside clock told him it was one o'clock in the morning.

"Raine?" he called.

When he received no answer, he rolled out of bed and went to look for her, but she was nowhere to be found.

What in the hell was going on, he wondered angrily. For some reason, Raine had gotten out of bed while he slept and gone out into the night. Whom was she meeting? And why?

The thought of her out alone at this time of night had him scared to death for her safety, and he had to force himself to remain calm and think rationally. Unfortunately, because of her damned secretiveness, he had no idea where she might have gone or how he might help her.

Helplessness was not a good feeling, he discovered. He needed to *do* something, and he decided to have a look around. A quick, efficient search of the flat soon had him in her closet. He pulled out a box, opened the flaps, and found himself staring at a Gauguin sculpture. Further search revealed a glittering emerald and diamond necklace, a Miró, a Reynolds, and finally the Pearls of Sharah.

Confused, dumbfounded, and slightly sick, he closed the closet door, crossed the room to the bed, and lay back down. Because of his profession, it was routine for him to skim reports and newspaper accounts of all crimes, and he recognized the Reynolds as a painting that had been stolen from Sir Hillary Colefield's collection some months earlier. And it was possible that the emerald and diamond necklace was the necklace that had been stolen two months before from Madame Françoise Guilbert's bedroom safe while she slept in her Paris pied-à-terre.

For several years a cat burglar had been on the loose in both England and Europe, and because he came and went without a trace and effortlessly eluded law enforcement agencies, he had been dubbed the Ghost.

Michael threw his arm across his forehead; his fist clenched and unclenched. He had always thought of the Ghost in masculine terms, but now . . . Could Raine possibly be the Ghost? It was hard for him to believe, but with the evidence staring him in the face—

No, she couldn't be. There had to be another explanation. A *reasonable* explanation.

The evidence in her closet demanded a radical alteration in all of his carefully thought out theories, but he couldn't seem to make his mind work. If Raine wasn't the Ghost, and he refused to believe she was, then she was somehow involved with the person who was. Who was he? And did the courier ring have something to do with the Ghost?

He closed his eyes. God help him, he didn't know what to do.

Sometime later, when he heard Raine open the front door of the flat, he still had no answers.

Raine peeked around the bedroom door and breathed a sigh of relief that Michael was still asleep. She wasn't up to answering his inevitable questions. On the way home she had devised a tentative plan; tomorrow she would go over it with Cameron. The plan frightened her; there were so many things that could go wrong. But she was determined to help her father.

Her love for Michael was thrilling—and more than a little overpowering. She needed time to find her feet with this new love. Eventually, she would have to tell him what she was doing. But her first order of business was to extricate her father from the predicament in which he had gotten himself.

Michael was an American businessman who seemed to see things in a straightforward manner, and she wasn't sure he'd be able to understand her father's logic in feeling that stealing art and jewels was the perfect sideline.

Her father needed her help. Michael needed her passion. When all was said and done, her loyalty to her father superseded her loyalty to Michael by many years.

She quickly undressed and carefully climbed into bed beside Michael.

He opened his eyes. "Hi," he said sleepily. "Where have you been?"

He was aware that she had just returned to bed, she realized anxiously, but did he know she had left the flat or how long she had been gone?

When she didn't answer, he touched her hair and whispered, "Your hair's damp. Did you go for a walk?"

"Yes."

He raised up on an elbow and looked down at her. "Why? It's rather late to be going for a walk, don't you think?" His voice was soft and without accusation.

"It was an impulse," she said, cringing inside because she was having to lie to him once again. "I couldn't sleep, and I've always loved to walk in the rain."

He pressed his lips to her forehead and tasted the rain. "I wish you'd awakened me. I would have liked to go with you."

"Next time I will." She put her hand to his face and ran her fingers down the rough skin of his jaw. He needed a shave. She needed him. *I'll tell him soon*, she promised herself. *I'll get things sorted out and then I'll confide everything to him.* She lifted her head and pressed her mouth to his. "Michael?"

"What?" He skimmed his hand up her stomach to her breast.

"I want to feel your mouth on every part of my body. Will you do that for me? Please . . ."

He felt himself tighten with sudden desire, and his long fingers closed convulsively around one taut, full mound. "Yes."

"And then I want you to make love to me. Will you? Slowly . . . and for a long, long time."

All the doubt, worry, and confusion in his mind receded to rest quietly and wait for a saner time to again rush forward. "What a request," he muttered huskily.

"Will you?" she persisted on a whispered breath.

"I don't know how you could stop me," he said, and ground his mouth down on hers.

Six

The pencil snapped in half. Disgusted at herself, Raine looked down at the two pieces in her hand. Evidently, her nerves were worse than she had thought. She tossed the two halves of the pencil into Cameron's office wastebasket, rose, and walked to the window. Without mentioning anything about her father, she had laid out her plan to Cameron. Her boss had been bewildered by her sudden interest in crime and justice, but when he had revealed that Interpol had one of their top men already here in London working on the courier theft case, she had insisted that the man be contacted. She glanced at her watch. According to Cameron, the inspector should be there soon.

Michael had left her flat early that morning, saying he had a meeting. Plans of her own had kept her from objecting. But she missed him.

Foolish, really, to miss him after being apart only a few hours. She smiled softly to herself. So she was foolish . . .

The door opened behind her. "Raine," Cameron said, "this is Inspector Carr."

She turned, and the polite greeting froze in her throat.

"Hello, Raine," Michael said.

Cameron glanced from one to the other. "You two know each other?"

Michael's gaze remained fixed on her. "We know each other very well, and if you don't mind, I'd like to talk to Raine alone."

"Certainly. Uh, if you need me, I'll be just down the hall." Cameron left the office, shutting the door after him.

Michael thrust aside the edges of his dark gray suit jacket and slipped his hands into his trouser pockets, leaving exposed a blue patterned shirt and tie. Completely at ease and in command, he walked slowly toward her. "So, you finally decided to take some action. That's good, Raine. There's just one thing. You didn't come to me, and I find that strangely hard to take." He stopped in front of her and lifted a hand to her head. Glistening pale blond hair fell like strands of sunshine through his fingers.

"You're an inspector with Interpol?" she asked in a shocked whisper.

He nodded.

"You've been *using* me?"

He hesitated a beat before he answered. "That

was only a small part of it, Raine. A *very* small part."

"You *used* me." A feeling of betrayal and pain layered her words, but a numbing cold invaded her body. It was like her relationship with Philip all over again; she hadn't been able to tell what either of the two men to whom she had given her heart had really wanted from her. "I feel so stupid," she said.

He framed her face with his hands and bent his head so that his eyes could look directly into hers. "Listen to me. I followed you that night into the Palm Court because I was attracted to you. I would have insisted on taking you home, *exactly as I did*, because I wasn't able to let you walk out of my life. I would have kissed you and continued to pursue you, *exactly as I did*, because there was simply nothing else I could do. I would have eventually made love to you, *exactly as I did*, because, Raine, I would have died if I hadn't."

She tried to pull away from him, but his hands kept her where she was. "I would have died," he repeated. "But an extra element was added to the situation when, that first night, I saw the pearls you were wearing and recognized them as belonging to a man who was a prime suspect in my investigation. From that point on, I had to find out as much as possible about you, the pearls, and who you were involved with, which, by the way, I *still* don't know. Who are you protecting, Raine?"

She jerked away, successfully freeing herself from

his grasp. A blinding anger surged through her and chased away the numbing cold. "Why do you want me to tell you, Michael? So that you can turn that person in? Just like I suppose you're going to turn me in." She hit her forehead for sarcastic emphasis. "Oh, how stupid of me. I'm sure you've already turned me in. Interpol must be very proud of you. Cameron said you were one of their top men, and no wonder. That overpowering charm of yours sweeps the women suspects off their feet and right under your spell, doesn't it? Then you have no problem taking them to bed, making love to them until they're senseless, and getting them to tell you anything you want to know."

"That method certainly didn't work with you, did it?" he asked, his own anger surfacing.

She threw up a hand. "You've got nothing to be ashamed of, Michael. I was completely under your spell. I had planned to tell you everything."

"Really?" he asked with blatant disbelief. "Then tell me now."

"Not . . . on . . . your . . . life."

He took hold of her arms and pulled her to him with a barely controlled violence. "Raine, you didn't listen to me. Our love affair would have followed the same path with or without those damned pearls. If you fell under my spell, honey, I felt like I'd been swallowed whole by you. Don't you know that?"

"I don't believe a word you're saying."

"Raine—"

"Why didn't you tell me who you really were?"

"It was for your own protection. I didn't and still don't know who you're involved with or how you fit into this whole network. If the wrong people had found out that you were seeing an Interpol investigator, your life would have been put into danger."

"As it was, the only danger I faced was from you."

"Danger? I was keeping you safe. Time and again I came up against evidence that would have told any other investigator that you were guilty as sin. But not me. Oh, no. I told myself that despite all the signs to the contrary, you were innocent."

"How open-minded of you."

His grip tightened on her arm and his teeth clenched. "I wasn't acting open-minded, Raine. I was acting like a man who had fallen hard for a siren with cool, rain-colored eyes and a body so hot I got singed every time I touched her. And just in case you're missing the entire point, here, let me tell you something else. If I had found out you were an ax murderer, I *still* would have fallen in love with you."

Her heart stilled. She had told him of her love for him, but he had never mentioned a word of love to her . . . only words of passion. *And, oh, what words of passion they had been.*

She tore out of his hold and moved around the room until Cameron's desk was between them. She was hurting badly. She was confused and angry. And she actually wanted Michael to take her in his arms and make love to her.

With painstaking thoroughness she cleared all emotion from her mind and heart and did what came naturally to her—she retreated behind a protective wall of reserve. "I suppose my request to work with another person from Interpol would be refused."

He took note of the change in her as she withdrew right before his eyes. He could try to reach into her, to reestablish the intimacy for which he was so desperate. But she obviously needed emotional distance from him, and, for the time being at least, he would give it to her. He deliberately masked the heat and intensity boiling inside him. "You suppose right."

"Very well, then, let's get on with it." She sat down, folded her hands atop the desk, and regarded him as if she were the president of a company and he were the vice-president. "Cameron said that he explained my plan . . . at least sketchily. What do you think of it?"

Unaffected by her businesslike demeanor, he settled his big frame into a chair in front of the desk and casually stretched out his long legs. "Not a hell of a lot."

"That's too bad, because I'm going to do it."

"Raine, you've got no idea what you're getting yourself into."

"I'll admit I've had no experience at this sort of thing. That's why I was hoping Interpol would help me."

"Interpol doesn't push babies into lions' cages."

"I'll do it with or without you, Michael. You make the decision which it's to be."

"You'll do *nothing* without me."

It took iron control not to fidget under his ice-blue gaze. "Then you'll help me?"

"I don't know yet," he said slowly, maintaining steadfast eye contact with her. "It depends on how honest you are with me."

"You're in no position to cast stones when it comes to honesty, Michael." It was out before she could stop it. "Never mind," she said quickly. "Don't respond to that."

"I wasn't going to."

She somehow managed to bank her flare of anger with a shrug. "My plan is simple, really. I'll go to the Ayers Club wearing the pearl necklace, and thereby attract Clinton Ayers's attention."

"You really think you need a pearl necklace to attract a man's attention?"

"It got yours, didn't it?" Her face was without expression, but her voice trembled slightly.

"I couldn't see the pearls in the fog, Raine."

She held up her hand, warding off memories and any further comments by either of them on a subject that was too personal and painful for her to contemplate at the moment. "I'm sorry. That was my fault. I shouldn't have said it."

"Maybe we'd do a lot better if we stopped thinking in terms of fault and blame."

She deliberately chose to misinterpret his remark. "You're right. We need to keep this conversation on a business level." She took a deep, cleansing breath. "Now . . . once I have Clinton Ayers's attention, I'll let drop information about important papers I'll be carrying. You'll make sure that I'm followed, or wired, or whatever it is that you people do, and Clinton Ayers will be caught red-handed."

"Why are you doing this, Raine?"

"To make sure he's put behind bars for the rest of his life."

"Why?" he asked again.

"Several of my friends and I are couriers. As long as this theft ring continues, we're in danger."

"You could walk away from this job anytime you wanted, and so could your friends."

He smiled at her, and she felt as if she were sitting in a straight-backed chair with a police interrogation light glaring in her eyes.

"It all comes back to this man you are protecting, doesn't it? So since you won't talk to me about him, let me tell you what I think is going on. Last night when you went out to meet him—"

"I didn't—"

"It's time to stop the lies, Raine. Yours. Mine. We've both been trying to protect, but it's time to face the damage we've done. And there has been damage done, hasn't there?"

"I don't want to talk about you and me. Let's get back to my plan."

"No, dammit." He leaned forward in his chair. "Let's get back to last night. While you were out, I searched your flat. Amid your designer dresses and custom-made shoes, I found art objects that had been reported stolen by a cat burglar known as the Ghost, who's been embarrassing us for several years now. After I recovered from the shock, I had to consider the possibility that you were the Ghost."

Her eyes widened with surprise. "Me?"

His grin was bleak. "It was a completely natural first assumption, which I discarded almost immediately. Still, I had to justify my assumption and prove to myself that my thinking wasn't based entirely on the fact that I was in love with you. So this morning I ran the dates you've been out of the country into the computer and tried to match them with the dates that the Ghost has struck. I'm thankful to say, there was no match."

"Really." Her voice was very small.

"Would you like a glass of water?"

His concern held a calculated note of condescension that sparked life from her. "If I want a glass of water, I'll get it myself, thank you."

He nodded, satisfied. "Having ruled you out as the Ghost, I remained confused. I had thought that Ayers's prize pearl necklace, you, and the mystery man you met in my hotel garden were all somehow connected to Ayers and the courier ring. And I couldn't figure out where or how the Ghost and the stolen art objects in your closet fit into the scheme of things. For a brief while I believed I had misjudged the whole thing. But then I realized that the Ghost and the mystery man in the hotel garden had to be one and the same person.

And that just because he stole artworks and jewels from rich and titled people didn't preclude him from being involved with the courier ring. Your coming to Cameron this morning with your little plan confirmed my new theory. You want Ayers caught because he is posing a threat to the Ghost. My guess is that he's blackmailing the Ghost."

All the color washed out of Raine's face.

He'd give anything if this scene didn't have to be played out, Michael thought, watching her carefully. When after a moment some of the color had returned to her face, he went on. "There are still several things I don't know for sure, but the question that continues to eat away at me is who the Ghost is to you."

"You're so smart. Surely you must have developed a theory." She arched her brow in a way that indicated she was only humoring him by asking.

He smiled to himself. The beautiful young aristocrat, cool and restrained, was back, covering the vulnerable, passionate woman he had come to love. "Oh, I have a theory all right. I've always known that this person you were protecting was someone very important to you, and that made me half blind with jealousy. But when we made love, it suddenly no longer mattered to me that there was another man out there somewhere who was important to you. Because I decided that you couldn't feel the same way about another man as you do about me. There was too much abandon and hunger between us for there to be room in you for two sets of the same kind of feeling." He paused. "Tell me I'm wrong."

The sudden switches between the business of her plan and their personal relationship was keeping her off balance. She swallowed a painful lump in her throat. "Would you believe me?"

"I know what I said is true."

"Then why ask?"

"Because I'm trying in every way I know how to break through to you and get you to react to me as someone you know a hell of a lot better than you're trying to pretend. Don't you see? It's impossible for you and me to keep our personal feelings out of this. Remember how close we've been. Confide in me."

"I don't trust you anymore, Michael."

"Oh? Would you like to tell me about trust, Raine? When a man goes into his lover's closet and finds a fortune in stolen artwork and jewels, trust would be justified in going right out the window, don't you think? Except, as I've already told you, I always believed that whatever your involvement was, it was innocent."

"How magnanimous of you."

"Or stupid. Since it seems you don't return the understanding."

She gripped her hands together so hard, her knuckles turned white. "Understanding? My life has been pretty much turned upside down in the past few days, Michael, but I think the biggest shock has been that you used me. Now that I've said that, I want to quit talking about you and me."

He sighed. He hated this; he *really* hated this. The desk between them might as well be a mile wide. She wouldn't let him reach her on any personal level. But, he vowed, she'd get over this feeling that she couldn't trust him, because she had to. He just wouldn't accept any other idea. He had no intention of losing her.

He stood, then perched on the corner of the desk, his body facing her. "This could be easier, you know. All you have to do is tell me what I need to know." He paused for a moment, but she remained impassive and silent. "Okay, then, we'll do it the hard way. Let's see. I know that you're very close with Edward Willoughby, but somehow I can't see him roaming over the roofs of castles and great homes. So the Ghost is probably a relative. Now, you've already told me that you're an only child. And your mother lives in Kentucky with her horses. That leaves your father." He eyed her thoughtfully. "I seem to recall you saying that you adored him, but that the two of you lead separate lives. That makes me conclude that the Ghost is your father." He leaned toward her. "How did I do?"

"Leave my father out of this."

"He's in it, isn't he?"

Trembling and white, she pushed away from the desk and stood. "Are you going to turn him in?"

For the first time, he dropped his gaze from

hers, because his answer was going to hurt her. "He's wanted in five countries, Raine."

"That doesn't answer my question. You want me to trust you, Michael. Prove to me I can. Tell me you won't turn my father in."

He raised his gaze and looked straight into her beautiful eyes. "I can't tell you that."

"Damn you." She grabbed for her purse and headed for the door.

He caught her and pulled her against him. "Where are you going?"

She hated herself for the need that sprang up inside her at the smell and feel of his hard body. "Away from you."

"But, you see, I won't let you."

"What are you going to do? Handcuff me to you?"

"If that's what it takes."

"You're a bastard."

"Maybe I am. But I'm also a man who's in love with you. Dammit, Raine, don't fight me. I can't stand it."

"I have to fight you, because I can't tolerate the thought of my father going to prison. He'd die there."

"Then why in the hell does he steal?"

"You'd have to know him to understand. He's never looked at the world quite like everyone else. He thinks earning extra money this way makes perfect sense, and he genuinely believes that he doesn't hurt anyone. Don't turn him in. Please."

He released her and unconsciously formed his

hands into fists. "Do you have any idea what you're asking me to do?"

"He's my father, Michael. What if he were yours?"

He let out an expletive that he normally wouldn't have considered using, but then, this wasn't a normal situation. "I can't tell you what you want to hear, Raine. But I can make a deal with you. I won't tell anyone what I know about your father until I know more about the situation."

"Does that mean there's a chance you'd let him go free?" she asked hopefully.

He stared at her, his expression brooding. "The problem is, I'd do just about anything in the world for you. I have to be careful that I don't forget what's important."

"It's a two-way street, Michael," she said softly, solemnly. "I have to be careful too."

When she walked into the sitting room of her flat from her bedroom that evening, Michael was struck speechless at how beautiful she was and how much he wanted her. She wore a long white sheath made of a silk jersey material that followed her curves the way his loving hand would. The dress made her look sexy, yet at the same time enhanced her elegance and sophistication.

All he could see of the necklace was the pearl clasp that rested at the base of her throat.

Seated in a comfortably cushioned chair, he nodded. "Very nice."

"Thank you," she said, and turned.

It was then he saw that the dress was cut to below her waist. And the pearls spilled in gleaming splendor down her naked back, knotted once in the center of her spine.

"You can't wear that," he muttered.

She glanced over her shoulder. "I thought you said it was very nice."

"The idea was to entice Clinton Ayers with the pearls, not make him want to strip off your clothes and rape you."

She turned back. "I hardly think he'll do that. We'll be in a club full of people."

He came out of the chair. "This is a bad idea. I'll use a trained agent."

"We went through all of that earlier. There's no one who can walk into that club tonight wearing these pearls and have the same impact. My credentials are impeccable. I'm a courier and a respectable member of society. He'll see the necklace, and he'll learn who I am. Whether or not he makes the connection with Father doesn't matter, because he's safely hidden away. The important thing is that Clinton will go crazy trying to figure out a way to get the pearls back. Then he'll learn that I'm the courier who will be carrying the information he's been waiting for. And he'll devise some way to get both."

With one hand on his hip and one finger pointed at her, he said, "There's one major flaw in your plan, Raine. You think the pearls are the bait, but in reality you're setting *yourself* up as the bait."

She kept her gaze steady, but inside she felt as

if she were crumbling. Tonight he had teamed black trousers and leather jacket with a black patterned shirt and tie. He seemed larger than life and he had a sensual power that reached across the room to her. "How many men are you going to have there tonight?"

"Five, counting Nigel, my man on the inside."

"Six counting yourself." She picked up her beaded evening purse. "I think I'll be well protected."

Against his better judgment, he went to her. "I know there's an argument somewhere that I should use against you, but, dammit, you fog my brain. I want like hell just to hold you."

She caught herself as she was about to sway against him. "No, don't. Please."

He knew they should leave. His men were already at their posts, waiting on them. "You can't be wearing a bra or, for that matter, panties. There's no place under that dress for anything but skin, and I want to touch it."

She moistened her dry lips with her tongue. "No."

He was driving himself crazy, but he couldn't stop. He lifted his hand and held it in the air between them. "If I put my hand on your back, I could slide my hand under your dress and in less than a second have your breast in my hand."

She should step away, she told herself. She should walk to the door, open it, and leave. But she made the mistake of looking at his big hand, and she saw that it was trembling. She closed her eyes.

"Do you have any idea how much I want you?" he asked, his voice gritty with desire.

Her eyes flew open, and she blinked away tears of reaction. "Yes," she whispered, "because no matter what's happened between us, I want you too. But we can't make love, because if we do I'll forget about helping my father. And I'll forget that you may very well send him to prison. But when we stop making love, I'll remember. And then I'll hate both of us."

"You're tearing me apart, Raine."

She blinked again, and this time a lone tear escaped from her eye and rolled down her cheek. "What do you think you're doing to me?"

He caught the tear on the end of his finger and pressed his thumb and forefinger together so that he absorbed her tear into his body. "All right," he said softly. "All right. I'll go along with you until the time comes when I can't. Then I'm going to make love to you, so long, and so hard, and so good, that you'll be too weak to tell me no."

Clinton Ayers surveyed the crowd in his club. There were many people there tonight he had never seen before, including the big tan-haired man dressed in black at Nigel's table. *Interesting.* He would do well to keep an eye on the man and the others. Not that he was adverse to new customers. It was just that he liked to know who was playing at his tables, and there was something about these men . . .

His gaze came to rest on Amanda Radford, then deliberately moved on as if she didn't exist. Their night together had been boring, so boring that he had played a few of his little games with her. Surprisingly, she had taken to them with enthusiasm, but he still hadn't received satisfaction.

He lit a long brown cigarette and drew hard on it, pulling smoke into his lungs. Regretfully, the nicotine didn't calm him as it once would have. Since the Pearls of Sharah had been stolen from him, nothing could calm him. Not even the success of his club. Not even sex.

From the moment he had seen the pearls in the home of a business acquaintance, he had known he must have them. The man had showed them to him with pride and had told him of their history and legend. The man had said they couldn't be possessed, but Clinton had known he *would* possess them.

As he had held them in his hands, he had been fascinated by their unearthly beauty. Curiously, their warmth and weight had soothed him. He had made a handsome offer, but the owner of the pearls had stubbornly refused to sell them. So he had killed the man and taken the necklace.

For two years he had possessed the pearls, using them as some people did a rosary. He had shown them to only a few select people, and had spent many a happy hour holding them and touching them. Then they had been stolen from him.

And ever since, there had been a black rage inside him that could not be assuaged. Nothing had ever obsessed him as much as the incomparable beauty of the Pearls of Sharah, he thought, taking another draw on his cigarette.

Nothing.

Then he turned and, through the crowd, saw her, and he felt the breath leave his chest.

She was the most beautiful woman he had ever seen. And she was alone as far as he could see. She had stopped at one of the tables to observe the play. Her pale blond hair was twisted up into an elegant chignon. The white silk dress she wore skimmed a body that made his blood turn hot. Her every movement was a study in grace. Good Lord, *who was she*?

He gestured abruptly for Tully. "Who's the woman in white?" he asked when the redheaded man was by his side.

Tully followed his boss's gaze to the woman. "I've never seen her before."

"Do you know if she came in with anyone?"

"Not that I noticed. Do you want me to see if I can find out who she is?"

"No," Clinton snapped curtly, "I'll do it myself."

Tully regarded his boss curiously. He wasn't sure whether Ayers's interest in the woman was a good sign or not, but he wanted to think it was. Tully had joined Ayers's organization because Ayers had struck him as a smart man and one with whom he could make a lot of money. But since that necklace had been stolen, Ayers had gotten sidetracked. He seemed to have forgotten about finding out when and where that packet would be shipped to Milan. And to make matters worse, now Reginald St. Clair had disappeared. "Is there anything else, boss?"

"Just one other thing. Watch out for Amanda Radford. The last thing I want tonight is a scene."

He crushed out his cigarette and started toward the woman in white. She turned away to move to another table. That was when he saw the pearls spilling down her back—*his* pearls—and he froze.

Her skin had a flawless, translucent sheen and a soft, velvety quality to it. Against this perfect backdrop, his pearls gleamed with a shimmering, opalescent light that seemed to beckon him to them.

A surge of lust tore through him, and he wasn't certain whether it was for the woman or the pearls. In his mind they had suddenly become one.

He compelled himself to maintain a leisurely pace as he strolled across the club. He even managed to stop now and then to speak to someone, but he always kept his eye on the woman in white. He barely noticed that Amanda stepped in front of him, blocking his path and attempting to gain his attention, or that Tully whisked her quickly away. When he finally came up behind the woman, he hid his excitement beneath a smooth, polite exterior. "Pardon me."

Raine turned. "Yes?"

He held out his hand to her. "I don't believe we've met. I'm Clinton Ayers."

"How do you do. I'm Raine Bennett." She put her hand in his.

"I'm delighted to meet you. And grateful."

She glanced down at their still joined hands. "Grateful?"

"Your beauty enhances Ayers's."

"Thank you very much."

"It's only the truth. This is your first time here, isn't it?"

"Yes." His skin was very brown; his fingers were lean and strong. His touch made her skin crawl. She extricated her hand from his and smiled graciously at him. "I'm enjoying it very much."

There was nothing obvious about her, he thought. Rather, she had a refinement and cool sophistication that were infinitely alluring. Her name meant nothing to him, but she affected him like no woman had in a long time. And the necklace she wore meant everything. "You must allow me to show you around, and in return, perhaps you could tell me about the remarkable necklace you're wearing."

"Necklace?" she asked with what she hoped was a convincing blankness.

"The pearls." He touched a finger to the heart-shaped clasp, then followed the line of the necklace around her neck and down her back, stopping at the knot of pearls at the center of her spine. "The pearls," he repeated.

She only just managed to control her shudder of revulsion at his touch. "I bought them from a man on the street. They're not real, of course, but I thought they were amusing."

"Amusing? Yes, I suppose they are." His hand tightened on the pearls.

Raine felt the pressure of the necklace pulling against her neck as if it were a rope being used to strangle her, and, for a moment, she panicked. Clinton Ayers was tall and lean—not big and muscled like Michael. But his touch was much harder. She didn't think she could have gone on if Michael hadn't been just a short distance away, his presence lending her courage.

Slowly, Clinton eased his grip on the pearls. "You say you bought them from a man on the street? That's a remarkable thing to do."

She forced her lips into an enticing curve. "I enjoy doing the remarkable."

His eyes darkened. "I enjoy women who do the remarkable."

She laughed softly. "Then we should get along well together."

"I think so," he murmured, then abruptly changed the subject. "Do you know anything about gaming?"

"Not really," she replied.

Clinton smiled. "Ah, a beginner. That means you'll probably clean me out tonight. Why don't we start with roulette?" He skimmed his hand beneath the pearls until his palm lay flat against her back, and guided her toward the roulette table.

At the blackjack table Michael indicated to Nigel that he wanted another card, and all the while, his anger was building. The animal had his hands all over Raine. God, how he hated this whole plan.

And he still wasn't certain it was even going to work. Clinton Ayers was a smart man. Raine was going to have to be very, very careful. If something went wrong . . .

Raine leaned over to place a bet. Clinton's hand slid intimately down her spine and stopped below her waist, the tips of his fingers resting just inside the white silk jersey of the dress.

A few feet away a betting chip snapped in half between Michael's fingers.

Clinton embraced Raine. "What did I tell you about beginner's luck? You won."

"How lovely," she said softly, and sank her teeth into her bottom lip to keep from screaming. She hadn't known playing up to him would be so hard. He was a very attractive man with a blatant sensuality that would be irresistible to most women. But disgust and revulsion were churning in her stomach, and she was very much afraid she was going to be sick if she didn't get away from him soon.

"Excuse me, Mr. Ayers," Tully said.

Clinton turned, his irritation plain as he snapped, "What is it?"

"There's a long distance call for you."

"Take a message."

"It's the call from Italy that you've been waiting for." It was Tully's hope that this call would rekindle Ayers's interest in the Milan packet.

Clinton stared indecisively at Raine for a moment. "Will you wait for me?"

"Of course."

He ran his hand down her arm, lightly brushing the side of her breast. *Lord, but she intrigued him.* "I won't be long."

Raine waited until Clinton disappeared into his office, then turned and walked straight out the front door of the club, leaving behind her pile of chips.

Taken by surprise by her abrupt action, Michael followed her as quickly as he could without causing comment. But by the time he reached the front steps of the club, all he could see were the taillights of a taxi disappearing down the street.

Seven

Michael frowned as he saw the front door to Raine's flat standing partially open. He entered, shut the door behind him, and locked it. "Raine?" he called, but received no answer.

His concern deepened when he saw her high-heeled pumps lying in the middle of the hall floor. In the parlor, her white dress rested in a heap on the carpet. And a few feet away, at the door to her bedroom, the pearls lay coiled like an exotic snake.

Sounds of running water from the bathroom drew him forward. Pushing open the door, he saw Raine, and his heart turned over. She was sitting in a tub of steaming hot water, scrubbing at her body with a large bath sponge.

He went to her and knelt down by the side of the tub. "What are you doing?" he asked softly.

She didn't look at him. "Getting clean."

"I know how you must feel. It killed me watching that vermin putting his hands on you."

"I can't reach my back," she said, a distressed expression on her face, her voice trembling.

He took off his jacket, tossed it aside, and rolled up the sleeves of his shirt. Then he took the sponge from her hands. "I'll wash your back."

"Use soap," she instructed.

"I will." He lathered her back and drew the sponge over her skin in gentle, soothing strokes. "Listen to me, Raine. You don't have to go through with this. We can stop it right now."

"You have to scrub hard," she said.

"Did you hear me? You don't ever have to see him again. We'll find another way."

She turned to look at him. "Did *you* hear *me*? You have to scrub hard."

He threw the sponge down and took her face in his hands. "Scrubbing the skin off your body is not going to help, honey."

Tears sprang into her eyes. "Then what will?"

"Come here." He stood and pulled her out of the tub. When she was on her feet, he wrapped a large towel around her, then lifted and carried her into the bedroom and to the bed.

He settled himself beside her and took her into his arms. "It's over, Raine. You're out of it."

"He knows who I am now."

"You'll be protected until the case is over."

She pressed her face against his chest and listened to the strong, steady beat of his heart and let the warmth of his body flow into her. Strangely, just hearing him say that she could quit gave her the courage to continue, and slowly, she grew calmer. "I'm sorry. I'm being a child about this."

"You have every right."

"No, I'm being foolish. It's just that I've never been exposed to a situation like that before."

"Thank God you haven't. No one should have to be."

She was silent for a minute. "I'm not going to quit. I'm staying in."

"No, Raine—"

"Yes. I have to. Ayers knows I have the pearls now, and he's not going to stop until he has them back. Besides, I'm the best bet you have to wind this up quickly. I'm the only courier who can draw him out. If you use anyone else, he's going to send his men after the packet. But with me and the pearls involved, he'll come after the packet himself, thinking he can get everything he wants at once."

The damned thing about it, he thought, was that she was right. He gently combed his fingers through her hair.

"And once you have him safely put away," she said, her voice gaining strength, "I can be assured that he won't force my father to steal any more art for him." She felt him stiffen at the mention of her father. "Don't worry," she said, "I won't ask you if you're going to turn him in. Not tonight. I just want you to hold me for a little while."

"I'll hold you for as long as you like."

• • •

Late that night, in the Ayers Club office, Tully sat across from Clinton and watched to see what effect his news would have.

"So, Raine Bennett is the daughter of Lord St. Clair. Well, well, what do you know."

"She's obviously playing some kind of game with you," Tully said.

Clinton idly fingered the stack of chips Raine had left behind. "I like games." He glanced at Tully. "She's a beautiful lady, don't you think?"

"I think she's dangerous. And I think we should find out what *kind* of game she's playing before you have any more to do with her."

Curiosity flickered across Clinton's face. "What is this? You've never shown disapproval before for anything that I wanted."

"It's just that nothing good has happened since those pearls were stolen. Then St. Clair's daughter coolly walks into the club wearing them. I tell you, it gives me a real bad feeling. Also, there were several strange men here last night. I—"

"Interpol."

"What?"

"I'm pretty sure at least one of them was an Interpol agent."

Tully sat back in his chair. "Hell."

Clinton smiled. "There's nothing to worry about. I'm too smart for them."

"Boss," Tully said, taking time to choose his words with care, "you've been able to operate a long time without detection, but if those were

Interpol agents, then they're obviously on to you, and they may be using Raine Bennett to trap you. Raine Bennett and those pearls."

"*My* pearls, Tully. They're *mine*, and I'm going to get them back."

"Sure, sure," he said soothingly. "Eventually, you'll get them back. But for now, why don't you play it cool? Do nothing."

Clinton came up out of his chair. "Don't be ridiculous. That phone call last night reminded me the papers we've been waiting for are due at any time to be carried to Milan. I can steal the papers, the pearls, *and* Raine right out from under their noses. Don't you see? It's all going to work out."

What Tully saw was that Clinton Ayers had lost all perspective. He was smart enough to see the trap that was closing around him, but he was crazy enough to feel he could escape it. He'd go along with him as long as it was profitable, Tully decided, but as soon as things started going sour, he was going to bail out.

Clinton stood and walked around the desk to Tully. "Until Raine and Interpol make their next move, we have other matters we have to take care of. There's someone working for me that I've had my eye on, and I think the time has come to take care of him. Here's what I want you to do. . . ."

The next morning Michael walked into Cameron's office and nodded to Raine, who had propped herself against the desk. "I'm sorry I'm late."

"That's all right. I haven't been waiting long."

He closed the door behind him. "I'm glad you're alone. I didn't want to have to ask Cameron to leave his office again, but the fewer people who know what's going on the better."

"Cameron understands that. Why did you want me to meet you here?"

"I'll explain in a minute. Right now I've got to talk to you about something else."

The grim expression on his face made Raine turn cold with apprehension. "What is it?"

He crossed the office to her side. "Do you remember I mentioned to you that I had a man on the inside of Ayers's club? Nigel?"

"I remember."

"They found him this morning in an alley. He'd been shot twice and left for dead."

Raine shut her eyes. "Oh, no."

"Ayers obviously figured out who he was. He might even have had him spotted right from the first. Nigel was never able to get close to Ayers, and the only important piece of information Nigel was able to come by was that Ayers was eager to get his hands on the packet scheduled for Milan. Its resale will be worth a bundle to him."

"You said Nigel had been left for dead. Does that mean he's in hospital?"

Michael nodded. "Yes. He survived the surgery, but it will be a while yet before we know whether he'll be all right." He reached down and pulled her to her feet. "Raine, the fact that Ayers figured out who Nigel was means he could also have figured out that Interpol is getting close. If it was dangerous for you to be in this before, it's three times as dangerous now."

"But you're not sure what he knows or doesn't know, right?"

"Raine—"

"I'm not backing out. For one thing, there's no way he can connect me with Interpol. For another, by keeping his mind occupied with me and the pearls, I can help your case."

"Think this over very carefully."

"Michael, if Clinton finds my father, he'll have him killed just like he tried to have Nigel killed. The doctors have given Nigel a chance. I want to try to give my father a chance."

"Oh, hell." His tone implied weary acceptance. "All right, Raine, but promise me you won't take any extra chances."

She smiled up at him, and it felt as if one of the weights had been lifted from his chest. Things were still a long way from resolved between them, but he'd take a smile for now and be glad for it.

"I promise," she said. "Now, why did you want me to meet you here?"

He still held her hands. "Let's sit down and I'll tell you what I've got in mind."

They had just taken their chairs when Edward Willoughby sauntered into Cameron's office.

A slight wrinkle in Edward's brow was the only sign he gave that he was surprised to see a strange man sitting in the chair beside Raine's. "Hello, luv. Do you have an assignment this morning too?"

She smiled. "Hello, Edward. No, I don't have an assignment. Do you?"

"I'm not sure. I was merely told to report. Where's Cameron?"

Raine cast a puzzled glance at Michael. "Are you behind this?"

He came to his feet and held out his hand to Edward. "I'm Michael Carr, Interpol."

The color drained out of Edward's face.

Raine stood too. "Michael, I refuse to let you bring Edward into this. I don't want anyone else I love being put in danger."

"That's just the problem, Raine. He's already in this. Why don't you take a seat, Edward."

"I think I'd better stand. Raine, what is all this?"

"I'm not sure." She looked at Michael.

He leaned back against the desk and stretched his legs out in front of him. "Edward, you're going to help us trap Clinton Ayers, and in the process you will be given immunity from prosecution."

"Immunity from prosecution?" Raine went to Edward. "What is Michael talking about?"

"I gather he's talking about the industrial espionage ring that has been preying on couriers for quite some time."

"But—"

"And he's found out that Clinton Ayers is behind it."

"Yes, I know that."

Edward had been staring at Michael, but now

he switched a pain-filled gaze to Raine, and he smiled gently. "Yes, I suppose you do, since you're here. But what you obviously don't know is that Ayers made sure that I lost heavily at his club, then blackmailed me into giving him information— dates, times, destinations of certain packets of documents."

"Oh, Lord, Edward, not you too." Instead of shock, she felt sorrow.

"You mean you . . . ?"

She shook her head. "Someone else close to me. Except he was being used in a different way."

"I didn't want to help Ayers, Raine. Once I even gave him false information, but when he found out, he threatened to let my father know about my debts. I suppose I should have told him to go ahead, but things are always more clear in retrospect, and at the time I considered that solution unthinkable. You know how my father is, Raine. I felt I had to hang on until I could see a way out. It didn't occur to me that my situation could get any worse, but it did. Ayers just kept pulling me in deeper and deeper."

"You don't have to explain anything to me. As I said, someone else close to me—someone who should have known better—became involved with Ayers in exactly the same way."

"I've really tried to get myself out of this, Raine, but . . . it's been hard."

Her eyes filled with sympathy. "I know." She turned to Michael. "Are you really going to give Edward immunity?"

"First he has to promise to cooperate."

"There's no problem there. I don't know what you have in mind, but I'll be glad to do whatever you ask. This has been a bloody nightmare." His mouth tightened. "I should have gone to the authorities myself, but I wasn't sure what they'd do to me."

Raine closed her hands around his arm. "Now you know, and you're doing the right thing by cooperating. He'll receive protection, won't he, Michael?"

Michael nodded."Yes."

Edward looked down at Raine. "I tried very hard to make sure that no courier was hurt because of what I told Ayers, but I wasn't always successful."

"I know you tried, though," she said softly. "No one who would spend weeks nursing baby birds and wounded animals back to health would want to see anyone hurt."

"The summers of our youth, eh?" He smiled sadly down at her, then his expression turned puzzled. "Raine, why are you here?"

"If you'll both sit down," Michael said, "I'll fill you in and lay out what I have in mind."

When Raine entered the Ayers's Club that evening, she paused in the doorway for effect, and the diaphanous layers of the pale pink silk mousseline of her dress swirled around her, then settled with seductive beguilement against her legs and ankles.

Clinton saw her immediately and threaded his way through the crowd to her. "Raine, I'm so glad to see you. And relieved. What happened last night? I was terribly disappointed when you disappeared on me."

She had already spotted Michael, sitting across the room at one of the tables, and with her courage bolstered, she was able to give Clinton her most charming smile. "It was terribly rude of me to leave like that, but I'd had a headache coming on all evening, and while you were gone, it suddenly reached the unbearable level. Since I didn't know how long your call would take, I decided that the best thing would be for me to go home. I hope you'll forgive me."

"I understand, and of course I'll forgive you." He bent over her hand and pressed a kiss on its back. When he raised his head, his eyes lingered on the Pearls of Sharah that were looped around her neck several times so that they formed a splendid bib over her breasts. Once again he wasn't sure if his lust for the woman could be separated from his lust for the pearls. It would be the ultimate ecstasy to make love to her while she wore them.

But she was out to ruin him, and so . . .

"You're an intriguing woman, Raine Bennett. And a beautiful one."

Putting just the right amount of surprise and gratitude in her voice, she murmured, "Why, thank you," as if his were the only compliment she'd ever received.

"Can I hope that you came back tonight to see me? Or did you perhaps come back to try your luck at the tables."

She lifted her hand and lightly touched his face. "You're the reason I'm here."

A hot hunger jolted through him, and for a moment he couldn't think. It took an inner struggle to get himself back under control. "Why don't we go into my office?" he said, his voice still not quite steady. "We'll be completely private there."

"I—" Raine panicked. She had meant only to flirt, not seduce him into wanting to get her alone.

"Raine, luv, what a surprise to see you here."

She freed herself from Clinton's grip and turned gratefully toward Edward.

"I never knew you liked to gamble," Edward continued.

"I never knew I did until last night."

"Did you win?"

She lifted and dropped one smooth shoulder. "Well, of course I did."

He laughed. "That's wonderful. Listen, a group of us are going out for drinks in a little while. Join us."

"I'm sorry, I can't. I have to go home early tonight." She glanced at her watch. "In fact, I really should be heading there now."

Clinton had been listening with barely concealed impatience to their conversation, but now he interrupted urgently. "You can't leave, Raine. You just got here."

"I know, but as I was about to tell you before

Edward came up, I dropped by for only a moment to see you and explain about my sudden disappearance last night."

His hand made an angry slicing gesture that took in her gown. "You dressed like that to come here and explain?"

She heard the suspicion and anger in his voice and smiled meltingly at him. "I had drinks at the Palm Court with an old friend beforehand."

"Why do you have to leave so early, Raine?" Edward asked right on cue.

She leaned toward him and, in a stage whisper, said, "I have to take that packet to Milan." To Clinton she gave a pretty shrug. "Business, you know. I'm leaving town tomorrow evening, and there are a great many things I have to do before then."

"I'm sorry to hear that, but if you really must leave now, then allow me to walk you to your car."

Edward reached for her arm. "Don't bother, Ayers. I'll see Raine out. I have a message for Raine from a mutual friend of ours."

Clinton stiffened. "You'll be coming back, won't you, Willoughby?"

Edward grinned cheerfully. "You couldn't keep me away."

Thirty minutes later Edward was seated in Clinton's office, watching a man clearly in a rage.

"Don't *ever* get in my way again," Clinton said, his teeth bared, his voice soft, "or you'll be very sorry."

"I apologize, but how was I to know you have a thing for Raine Bennett?"

Clinton's eyes narrowed. "You weren't going to tell me about the Milan delivery, were you?"

"Well, I—"

"No, you weren't. I wonder what else you haven't been telling me."

With small fidgety movements that were intentional, Edward shifted nervously in his chair. "Nothing. You know everything."

"I don't believe you, but I'll give you this one last chance to redeem yourself. I want to hear the details of the Milan trip right now."

"I'll tell you everything you want to know."

Raine had changed out of her long gown and donned a circular flowered skirt of orchid and mauve and a long, loose mauve sweater when Michael showed up on her doorstep.

"It looks like you have plans to go out."

"Yes, I do."

"It's rather late, don't you think?" he asked mildly.

"Don't start with me, Michael. My nerves are about shattered as it is."

"All the more reason not to go out." He paused. "You're meeting your father, aren't you?"

The angle of her head suggested a hint of defiance. "Yes."

"Then I'm going with you."

"You're mad if you think I'm going to let you."

"Raine, think about it for a minute. If you don't let me go with you, I'll follow you. Believe me, you'd never even know I was behind you."

"Thank you for telling me. I won't go."

"Won't your father be worried if you don't show up?"

"I'd rather he be worried than devastated that I brought an enemy to his hiding place."

"Raine, please don't see me as an enemy."

"How should I see someone who has the power to put my father in prison for a long, long time?"

"I do have that power. But, honey, let me tell you something. I long ago passed the point where I can be objective about you. I started putting my personal needs ahead of my professional obligations early on in this relationship."

She absorbed his biting but impassioned words. "I'm not sure I believe that."

He let out a long breath. "Look, I don't want to fight with you. Let's make a deal. Tonight I'll put aside the inspector side of me. When I meet your father, I'll simply be the man who is in love with his daughter."

She gnawed on her lower lip. Her father's future was at stake, and she wasn't certain she could trust Michael. "You won't use anything you learn tonight to apprehend or prosecute my father?"

"No."

She rubbed her brow. "I don't know—"

He lay his hands on her shoulders. "Honey, you're going to have to decide to trust me sooner or later, because I'm not going to go away. I love you, and I want to help you. And most of all I want to keep you safe. Now, are we going or not?"

She stared up into his eyes and rediscovered what she had known from the beginning. Ice blue described the color of his eyes, not the temperature. They were looking at her with a warmth and a tenderness and a concern that went a long way toward melting the hurt and distrust she had first felt when she had learned he had deceived her. "All right, Michael. You can come with me."

Michael drove and Raine directed him to the same coffee house in Elephant and Castle where she had met her father two nights earlier. When they walked in, Reginald was hard pressed to mask his surprise. "Raine?"

"Father, I'd like you to meet Michael Carr. He didn't like the idea of me coming down here alone this late at night."

Reginald rose and extended his hand to Michael. "I recognize you. You're the chap Raine met the other night in Green Park, aren't you?"

Michael cast a questioning glance at her, and she explained. "It was Father who was following me."

"I see. Well, then, I suppose I should thank you, Lord St. Clair. If Raine hadn't been so frightened, she would never have run into me, and we wouldn't have met."

"Call me Reginald, won't you? After all, you must be very important to Raine for her to bring you here."

They seated themselves around the table.

Michael glanced at Raine and noted she still wore a look of apprehension. He didn't blame her, but he also couldn't think of anything to do to reassure her. The evening would just have to play itself out. "I'd like to think I am. She's very important to me."

Reginald leaned back against the bench, and after giving Michael a thorough scrutiny, announced his verdict. "I'm glad to see that you look like a dependable fellow. After that bastard Philip Bennett, Raine needs someone who will cherish and care for her."

"Father!"

Reginald raised a warning finger at Michael. "She doesn't ride, you know, and you shouldn't make her."

Michael smiled inwardly. He felt like a young boy being lectured to by a protective father. But then, he was fast learning that Reginald was exactly that. In fact, it was hard for him to put together the image he had in his mind of the Ghost with Raine's flesh-and-blood father. "I would never think of forcing her to ride."

"Good, good. I'm relieved to hear it. Now, Michael, what exactly is it you do for a living?"

Raine groaned. "That's enough, Father. We're here to see how you're doing, not to have Michael cross-examined."

Reginald's look told her he thought her logic a bit off the mark. "But don't you see, darling, I'll be much better if I don't have to worry about you. And if Michael has a good, solid career going, that makes him someone in whom you can have all the more confidence, because he's established himself in life." He turned to Michael. "Money's important, of course, but not absolutely vital. Raine has plenty enough for both of you."

This time Michael did smile. "I'm not rich, but I do make a comfortable living, and I've made some good investments over the years." He glanced at Raine. "I'm an inspector with Interpol."

She had been dreading this moment and she hastened to reassure her stunned father. "Michael has promised me that he will not use anything he learns here tonight against you."

"Good Lord, you mean he *knows*?"

With a nod Michael answered Reginald's question for Raine. "I figured it out. And Raine's right. I did promise. You see, my job is to investigate Clinton Ayers and the industrial espionage ring he heads. In this case, Raine's and my interests correspond, because she's trying to free you from his blackmail."

Reginald immediately forgot his apprehension for himself. "What are you doing, Raine? If there is so much as a modicum of danger involved, I want you to stop immediately."

"There's no danger," she said, hoping her voice didn't betray any of her own doubt. "I'm simply using the pearls you stole from him as bait, then adding a particularly desirable packet of information as further enticement. He'll come after the pearls and the packet, and we'll have him."

"You forgot to add, he'll come after *you*," Reginald said perceptively. "I don't like this one bit. What do you think, Michael?"

Michael nearly chuckled. The Ghost was asking him for advice as if they were involved in something together. Abruptly, he sobered as he realized that they *were* involved in something together. They both loved Raine and wanted her safe.

"I admit that I'd rather trap Ayers some other way, but Raine is being protected, and by this time tomorrow, it will all be over."

Reginald tugged at his ear. "Well, I suppose it sounds all right, as long as I can rely on you to see that no harm comes to her. And I must admit it will be a relief not to have to worry about Ayers anymore." His look turned sharp. "Michael, I want you to know that no one has ever been hurt during any of my burglaries. I pride myself on the fact that I don't even carry a weapon. And no one suffers from my thefts. The people from whom I steal simply turn the loss in to their insurance company and are compensated, most of the time with a greater amount than the article I have taken is worth." His sudden beaming smile fell on both Raine and Michael. "It works out nicely all the way around, with everyone gaining."

"But they no longer have the pleasure of their painting," Raine said, feeling her father had missed a vital point.

"Bah! Most of the art is bought for investment purposes, not for appreciation of the work. It's incomprehensible to me, but there it is. The world is a funny place, eh, Michael?"

"Funny," Michael echoed, though he found not the least bit of humor in the situation. He couldn't imagine the dapper gentleman sitting across the table from him performing the daring deeds that reportedly had been done over the years by the Ghost. Reginald St. Clair appeared to be one of the most harmless people he had ever met in his life, along with one of the most likable. Yet he just also happened to be on Interpol's wanted list.

Eight

Raine remained silent on the drive home, and listened to the silence that came from Michael's side of the car. He had to have a lot on his mind. The whole of what would happen tomorrow, and whether or not it would be successful, rested on his shoulders. In addition, she knew that he was very concerned about her safety.

Then there was the problem of her father. She had no idea what his decision would be. She was aware that by asking him to keep quiet, she was asking him to betray the ethics of his profession and perhaps even break the law. By turning in her father, Michael would be doing right. By not turning him in, he would be doing wrong. But if he told Interpol what he knew, she would never be able to see him again. She couldn't take her happiness with the man responsible for her father's

unhappiness. Her position was very likely inde-
fensible, but then, emotions of the heart were
never logical.

Michael drew the car to the curb in front of her
flat and turned off the engine. She decided to
speak before he could say anything. "I don't want
to be alone tonight."

Through the dim interior of the car he could
see the soft shine of her pale blond hair as it fell
over her shoulders. "Are you frightened?"

"Yes."

"Good. People who are frightened are careful."

"People who are frightened also make mistakes."

"You won't have a chance. You'll be wired for
sound, and as soon as Ayers goes for the packet,
we'll close in."

"It sounds so easy." Her tremulous laugh touched
a tender spot in his heart.

"It's not easy, so you shouldn't feel bad about
being scared. You would never have even come up
with the idea if you didn't have courage. Come
on. I'll go up with you and go through your flat
just to make sure there are no surprises waiting
for you."

"Aren't you going to stay?"

He hesitated. "There's nothing to worry about.
He won't make a move until you have the packet."

"That's very reassuring," she said, her tone dull.
She had asked him to stay because she needed
the comfort of his presence, the heat of his body,
the strength of his arms, and, most of all, his
love. But quite obviously he didn't want to stay.

In her flat Michael went through all the rooms, then came back to her with a report. "Everything's fine. You should be able to rest well."

She drew herself erect to hide her hurt. "I'm sure you're right. I'll be just fine."

He put out a hand to her but quickly drew it back. He pulled a pad from his jacket pocket and jotted down a number. "If anything frightens you, call this number. They'll reach me wherever I am."

She took it from his outstretched hand. "Thank you." She stared down at the piece of paper, not even seeing the numbers written on it. "Where will you be?"

"I'm not sure. Probably at the hotel."

She nodded, her hair falling around her face to conceal her anguished expression. "I'm sure I won't have to use the number."

A sudden hand beneath her chin raised her face. "What's wrong, Raine?"

"Why don't you want to stay here tonight?"

"Good Lord, don't you know that I want to stay here more than anything else in the world? But if I did, I'd do a damn sight more than protect you."

The loud drumming of her heart prevented her from hearing the word she spoke next. "Stay."

Every muscle in his body tensed, and he studied her intently. "Are you sure, Raine? Because if you're not . . ."

"Stay," she repeated.

He needed her badly, yet he drew her to him slowly. "I want this loving to last a long, long time," he murmured.

She understood. They both knew that their future was uncertain. After tomorrow it was possible that they would both be alone. But tonight was theirs. She raised her arms and wound them around his neck. "We'll make it last all night."

He lowered his mouth and lightly touched her lips. His chuckle fanned warm breath against her lips. "I don't know about all night. When I'm with you, there's a certain point when my mind shuts down and my body takes over." He pulled her tighter against him and pressed into her. "Feel that? It's already starting to happen."

"Then maybe we should go to bed."

"Hell of a good idea."

Arm in arm they made their way into the bedroom. Beside the bed, they stopped.

"Undress me," she whispered. "All the way, *before* we get into bed."

He slid his hands beneath her sweater, then up, until he could close his fingers around her bare breasts. "You didn't wear a bra."

"Sometimes I don't."

"Like the other night. God, how I wanted you." His thumbs flicked at her nipples.

Her full lips parted on a gasp as the tips of her breasts hardened. She had to grasp his shoulders to keep from falling. "I wanted you too."

His hands caressed her, and his thumbs repeatedly brushed over her nipples. "I can almost feel you swelling against my hands."

"I thought you were going to undress me." Her eyes were half closed and the color of smoke.

"I'll get around to it." He pushed her sweater up until it was bunched over her breasts. "But first I've got to have a taste of you." He bent his head and sucked a stiffened peak into his mouth. The pulling action was very sure and made heat melt between her legs.

"You're exquisite," he muttered, then switched to the other breast.

Everything ceased to exist for Raine except the man bent to her, his mouth creating sensations in her that made darkness light and brightness dim. "Michael, you're either going to have to stop that or we're going to have to lie down."

"What else do you have on?" he asked, his tongue licking at the upright nipple.

"Flats." She stepped quickly out of them.

He laughed, then softly bit at her. "That's not fair. What else?"

"This skirt."

"How does it come off?"

"There's a button . . . on the side. And a zipper."

Without removing his mouth from her, he undid the button and unzipped the orchid and mauve skirt. It slid down and came to rest on the curve of her hips. He pushed his hand beneath the skirt and panties and took hold of her bottom. "I wanted to do this the other night when you had on that low-backed dress," he said, sucking, talking, and kneading her bottom all at the same time.

Her chest felt tight; she couldn't breathe. "Lord, Michael, what are you trying to do? Punish me?"

"Maybe. Promise me you'll never wear that dress for anyone else but me."

"I promise," she said, her voice soft and husky.

He raised his head and brought his mouth down on hers with force and possession. Only he didn't hold her. As he thrust his tongue as deeply as possible into her mouth, he hastily undressed himself. When he was completely naked, he pulled her against him so that her nipples were pressed hard against his chest, and an animallike sound came from his throat. "I've already tasted you and held you in my hands. Now I need to feel you."

"And I need more," she whispered.

He smiled. "You said you wanted it slow. You're going to get it slow."

She made a soft, whimpering sound, but he didn't hurry as he pushed her skirt and panties down until they fell around her feet. He lifted her out of them, and she wound her legs around his hips, holding herself tightly to him.

"You're definitely not playing fair," he said in a voice little more than a growl. He started kissing her neck while running his hand down the ridge of her spine.

"I know, and I can't even say I'm sorry." Her words were mere breaths as she moved her lower body against his.

His brain was slowly shutting down, but he desperately wanted to draw the torturous pleasure out. He took the delightful mounds of her bottom into his hand and lifted her slightly, then let her fall.

She threw back her head with a moan. The hair on his body was erotically rough, and as he moved her against him, nerves began to burn with excruciating sensitivity.

"We can't make love yet. You still have your sweater on."

"Take it off."

With his hands still gripping her bottom, he pulled her lower body against him. "My hands are full."

"Then I'll take it off." She released one arm at a time from the mauve sweater, then worked it over her head and threw it as far as she could. It hit the opposite wall and slid down to the carpet. "Now we're both undressed," she said. "Let's go to bed."

"Great idea."

Wrapped around him as she was, he felt they were one person, and he carefully lowered them both to the bed. Only then did she pull her legs from around him.

He positioned himself over her, but with iron control he held himself away from her. Sweat lightly covered his body, testament to his effort. He dipped his fingers between her legs. Closing her eyes, she arched her hips upward, and he felt the sweet moistness that was waiting for him. Unable to stop, he delved deeper, experiencing in this unique way what he would soon know in another way.

She was drugged and hurting with her need for him. Her eyelids felt weighted; her throat felt closed. She barely was able to bring his face into focus and whisper, "Every time you touch me, it makes lightning inside me. But it's you I need."

His endurance was at an end. He slid slowly into her, joining the lightning, and drawing cries from both of them.

Later, right before they fell asleep, he murmured, "No one in the world makes love the way we do."

Across the street from Raine's apartment, the flare of a lighter illuminated the well-manicured hands of a gentleman, then lifted to light a long brown cigarette and show the face of an obsessed man.

The morning sun filtered around the edges of the mauve satin bedroom curtains. On the bed Raine curled close to Michael's big body and rested her head in the crook of his arm. "Do you have to go?" she asked. "Can't you stay just a little while longer?"

"I wish I could, honey." He looked down at her. "Don't be scared. Everything is going to be all right."

"I know. " She grimaced self-deprecatingly. "This was my idea, after all. I can't blame anyone but myself."

"I think you're wonderful. And tonight we'll drink champagne and celebrate."

"It's a date," she said softly.

He pressed a kiss to her forehead. "What's bothering you, honey?"

"Father—"

"Raine, for the rest of the day you can't afford to think of anyone but yourself and the part you'll be playing."

"I know, but—"

"You want to know if I've decided whether I'll turn him in, right?"

She nodded, staring up at him.

Lord, he thought, it was amazing what a pair of rain-colored eyes could do to a relatively strong and sane man. "Try to understand, honey. I've spent all of my adult life in law enforcement. I never wanted to do anything else." The slight roll of his shoulders indicated the bleak helplessness he was feeling. "There are a lot of things I need to consider. It's not an easy decision to make."

"I understand, and I want you to know that I don't feel good about what I'm asking you to do. I don't have any other choice. In the end, you won't either. You'll have to get up every morning and face yourself in the mirror, as I will."

The lifeless tone of her voice tore holes in his heart. "I'll tell you one thing, Raine. Whichever way my decision goes, I'm not going to let *you* go."

She stayed silent, because no matter what either of them wanted, she knew she wouldn't be able to face a future with a man who was responsible for putting her father away for what could be the rest of his life. She was as wrong in feeling this way as her father had been in stealing other people's possessions. But there was nothing she could do about the way she felt. She and Michael had to deal with their own consciences.

"Raine?" he asked, concerned.

"I'm all right."

"Are you sure?"

She nodded. "I'm sure."

"Okay, then. I guess it's time to go to work." He raised his arm and looked at his watch. "It's ten now. Edward told Clinton that your flight leaves at seven this evening. I judge you can expect a call from him—" The ringing of the phone interrupted him. "Speak of the devil." She reached for the phone, but his hand came down and covered hers, preventing her from lifting the receiver. "Do you know what to do?"

Her lips curved with dry humor. "I should. You've drilled it into me."

"Good girl," he said, and released her hand.

She lifted the receiver. "Hello?"

"May I speak to Michael?" a voice she had never heard before said.

"Yes, just a moment." She held the receiver toward Michael and whispered, "It's for you."

He took the phone. "Yes?" After listening for a minute, he said, "That's great. Thanks for calling." He hung up and smiled at her. "Nigel is going to be all right."

"Thank goodness. That is good news. Maybe we

can take his recovery as an omen that things will go well for us today. What do you think?"

"I think we should do exactly that." He leaned forward to kiss her, but they both jumped when the phone rang again. His smile faded. "This could be Ayers. Try not to sound nervous."

She gave a short laugh. "Easier said than done."

"I'm right here."

"I know." She picked up the receiver. "Hello?"

"Good morning, Raine. This is Clinton Ayers."

She cut her eyes to Michael. "Good morning, Clinton."

"I trust you slept well?"

"Very well, thank you."

"Good. The reason I rang was to ask you if you'd have an early supper with me at my flat."

"Oh, I don't know, Clinton."

"I know you said that you had a lot to do before you left town this evening, but I was hoping you could find time for me. We could even call it a late lunch, say about four or five?"

"Well . . ."

"Please say yes. We haven't really gotten a chance to know each other."

She hesitated for an appropriate amount of time. "I guess I could manage it."

"Wonderful. I'll send a car for you. I suppose you'll have to make a stop by your office and pick up the packet."

"No. It will be delivered to me earlier in the day."

"Well, then things will work out perfectly," he said cheerfully. "My car will pick you up at four, and we'll have our late lunch. Then I will personally accompany you to Heathrow to see that you get off safely."

"That sounds lovely."

"Oh, and, Raine?"

"Yes?"

"You will wear that amusing necklace of yours, won't you? You know, the pearls. I find them charming."

"If you like."

"Excellent. Then I'll see you a little after four. Good-bye for now."

"Good-bye." She hung up the phone and looked at Michael. "It's all set. His car will pick me up at four, and he asked me to wear the pearls."

Michael smiled. "He's falling into our trap beautifully." He rolled out of bed, reached for his clothes, and began dressing. "I have to leave for about an hour or so. When I come back, I'll have my men in position, and I'll wire you for sound."

A terrible sense of aloneness came over her, but she kept it to herself. "Don't be gone long."

"I won't." He stuffed the tail of his shirt into his trousers and reached for his shoes. Then he bent over the bed and placed a lingering kiss on her lips. "Don't worry about a thing."

Minutes later, from the backseat of his Rolls-Royce, parked down the street from Raine's apartment, Clinton Ayers watched Michael's Aston-

Martin drive off. His hand absently caressed the back of the car phone's gold receiver. "They think they've got me," he said to Tully, who was sitting in the front seat. "They think I don't know what's going on, but I'm smarter than the whole lot of them put together."

The man's mind was completely warped, Tully realized with concern for himself. Ayers paid him a good salary, but there was not enough money in the world to make him take a fall when there was no reason to.

"They were up there all night together, you know," Clinton said as if he were talking to himself.

The redheaded man looked over his left shoulder and pulled down his dark glasses. "Mr. Ayers, I think you should seriously reconsider your plan. Interpol is not to be taken lightly. They might have had those pearls stolen to throw you off balance."

Clinton's attention snapped back to the man in the front seat. "You don't know what you're talking about. As I see it, there's no way I can lose. I know what they plan, but they have no idea what I'm going to do. Playing cat and mouse with Interpol is a very exciting game. By the end of the day I'll have everything I want, and they'll have nothing."

Tully replaced his glasses, turned back around, and stared out the front windshield. "Yeah, sure."

Raine forced herself to eat a good breakfast,

and then took a long, leisurely bath. When her nerves had calmed somewhat, she climbed out of the tub, dried herself, and donned a silk wrapper. She told herself it would be senseless to dress until she had been wired for sound. But in truth, she knew that she was delaying for another reason. Once she was dressed, she would have nothing to do but watch the clock and count the minutes until Clinton's car would come for her.

Which was exactly what she was doing now.

She walked into the sitting room and switched on the stereo. Michael would be here soon, she assured herself, and then her nervousness would vanish. As if to prove her point, there was a knock on the door. She rushed down the hall and flung open the door. It wasn't Michael.

"Ms. Bennett." The young man who worked at her office nodded respectfully. "I was supposed to bring you this." He held out a leather folder.

"Yes, thank you."

Raine took the folder and shut and locked the door behind her. She stared down at the packet. The information was bogus, just another piece of bait in a trap. She prayed it would work.

Michael, where are you? I need you.

In his hotel room Michael paused in the middle of briefing his men and frowned. Something was bothering him, but he couldn't quite put his finger on what it was. Everything seemed to be going like clockwork, and Ayers was reacting as Michael had hoped. He had called Raine right on schedule, and had suggested a meeting with her as Michael had figured he would.

Two of his men had the Ayers Club under surveillance and two were watching the man's flat. If Ayers so much as looked as if he might go anywhere, Michael would be notified immediately. And when Ayers's car picked up Raine, the car would be tailed back to Ayers's flat, where every word Raine or Ayers spoke would be monitored. There was no possibility that Raine would be in any danger.

So what was bothering him?

He cast his mind back over the conversation he had overheard between Raine and Ayers this morning.

There was another knock on the door, and Raine flew to answer it. "Michael," she said as soon as she flung the door open.

"No," Clinton said as he brushed past her into the hallway. "Who's Michael?"

Raine stared at him, stunned. Something had gone very wrong. This wasn't in the plan.

"Raine?" he prompted.

"Michael is a friend of mine. I'm expecting him at any moment."

"A *close* friend?" he asked, turning to make his way down the hall and into her sitting room.

Raine followed him, but her mind was working

rapidly, trying to decide what to do. "Clinton, what are you doing here? I didn't expect you."

In the middle of the room he turned to her with a smile. "I know. I've taken you off guard, haven't I? But you haven't answered my question, so I'll have to assume that this Michael is an extremely close friend." His gaze took in her state of undress with an unconcealed greed. "You look very desirable."

She pulled the silk wrap closer around her. "I've had a rather lazy morning."

"Did you decide that all those things you said you had to do could wait?"

The shock had passed, leaving her with an intense awareness of danger. She licked her bottom lip with the tip of her tongue, and the minute she did, she wished she hadn't. The action drew his gaze. "If you'll excuse me, I think I'd better get dressed." There was a telephone in the bedroom.

"I think you look charming just the way you are. In fact, I think it's probably better that you don't dress."

Raine suddenly noticed something. Clinton appeared different. He was dressed in black as usual, but his clothes looked as if they'd been slept in. And there was an odd light in his eyes, almost as if he had a fever. "Clinton, are you feeling well?"

"I'm fine. Ah-ha . . ." His attention was caught by the leather folder that had been delivered to her a short time before. He went to it and picked it up. "I saw the boy bring this to you. I assume it's what you're supposed to be delivering to Milan."

"Please give it to me," she requested with as much authority as she could muster. "No one else is supposed to handle it. There's highly confidential information in the folder."

He stared at the folder thoughtfully. "I'd be very surprised if you were right, but we'll take it along with us anyway."

"Take it with us? What are you talking about?" He moved, heading for her bedroom. "Wait, where are you going?" She chased after him and found him standing beside her bed, staring down at it.

"This is where you slept with him, isn't it? *Michael*. I wasn't sure of his name. I wonder . . . do you suppose it's proper procedure for an Interpol agent to sleep with a woman who is involved in the case he is investigating?"

Cold fear kept her silent. He began to walk toward her, and she started to back away from him.

"Do you have any idea what it did to me to be outside all night, looking up here, watching your bedroom window, and imagining the two of you locked in passion?" His tone was rather mild; his eyes were ablaze with something not quite sane.

Raine's retreat was stopped at the wall, and then he was in front of her, his hand closing around her throat. "I'll tell you what it did to me," he said softly. "It excited the hell out of me. Imagination is a powerful thing, Raine. Powerful. Before it's all over, you're going to tell me in detail all the things he did to you."

"You're mad," she whispered.

"Mad for you." His thumb stroked the column of her throat. "Where are the pearls?"

She deliberated for perhaps five seconds. Maybe there was still a way their plan could be salvaged. If she could just keep him in the apartment until Michael returned. "They're in my closet."

He grabbed her wrist, dragged her to the closet, and opened the door. "Where?"

"There. In the corner," she said, happy to find that there were no tremors in her voice. "Please, let go of me."

He laughed excitedly, his gaze riveted on the box in the corner of her closet. "That's not in the plan, Raine."

One-handed, he retrieved the box and flipped up the lid. His indrawn breath was audible as he saw the gleaming pearls nestled against the black velvet interior of their case. "My God, I have them back." He released her and snatched the pearls out of the box, but she had time only to take a step before his hand clamped around her wrist again.

Mesmerized, he continued to stare at the pearls, and Raine used the time to sort through her alternatives. Her one hope rested in keeping his mind on the pearls and off her.

"They're extraordinary, aren't they?" she said, her voice low.

"Yes," he answered. "I've missed them." Slowly, his eyes switched to her. "You know, it was really remarkable, but when you wore them, they seemed to take on an added dimension."

Her plan had backfired. "No, I'm sure you're wrong. The pearls stand alone in their beauty."

"I've fantasized making love to you while you wore them. Did you know that?"

Ice slid down her spine, but before she could think of anything to say, he shrugged regretfully and went on.

"But I don't want you wearing them when I take you. I wouldn't want to get blood on them."

Her heart almost ceased to beat.

His grip on her wrist tightened. "Let's go. I have a car waiting."

Nine

Michael was a block away from Raine's apartment when he looked down the street and saw Ayers force Raine into the back of his Rolls.

"Dammit!"

He hit his steering wheel with the flat of his hand, then immediately pulled his car to the curb and radioed to the two cars following his. "Ayers has Raine. I'm going to stay well back and follow them. You two parallel him on the side streets as long as you can, then fall back in behind me. Any questions?"

"Why don't we just surround the car?" a disembodied voice said. "There are enough of us."

"Negative. We have to go under the assumption that he's armed, and surrounding them could endanger Raine and automatically set up a hostage situation."

"All right, then. We'll be close by. Let us know if you lose him at a red light."

In his rearview mirror Michael saw the two cars turn off the street, one going left and one going right. "Stay on your toes," he said into the radio, aware that he was speaking more to himself than he was to his men. "I don't want anybody screwing up."

He had made a very critical mistake. He prayed it wouldn't be fatal for Raine.

Raine had never been so frightened or felt more alone. She was no longer thinking how to entrap Clinton, but rather how to stay alive. She had already decided that the red-haired man who was driving the car would be no help. He hadn't even looked back once.

Beside her, Clinton fingered the pearls as if he were receiving sustenance from them and his very being depended upon touching them. He hadn't spoken to her since he'd pushed her into the car, and she might have thought that he had forgotten her, except, while he held the pearls in one hand, he kept a tight grip on her wrist with the other.

When she had first met him at the club, she had known he was dangerous and that she should be extremely cautious. What she hadn't known or been able to see was this terrifying menace that was now oozing from him.

Trying not to draw his attention to her, she

gazed out the window. Their destination remained a mystery to her. They had been on the M1 for about forty-five minutes now, heading north, away from London. She hoped wherever they were going was a great distance away. As long as the car kept moving, she was safe. Once the car stopped, she knew the fight for her life would begin.

When the big car turned off onto a road, Raine broke into a cold sweat. Then all too soon the car veered into a lane, and not long afterward came to a stop in front of a secluded cottage.

Clinton focused his dark, feverish eyes on her. "We're here. How do you like it? I bought it not too long ago, thinking it might come in handy." Without waiting for her to answer, he opened the door of the Rolls and dragged her into the cottage.

With repeated glances over his shoulder the red-haired man followed more slowly.

Inside, Clinton shoved her to the couch. "Tully, where are you?"

"Here," Tully said, stepping into the room.

"Things worked out well, didn't they?" His smirk contained an arrogant invincibility.

"I don't think we can say that for sure yet," Tully replied cautiously, his eyes darting to Raine, then back to Clinton.

"Certainly we can. I told you I would outsmart Interpol, and that's exactly what I've done. I have Raine, the pearls, and the packet. However, I don't think it would be wise to count my money quite yet on the sale of the information inside." He tossed the leather folder to a table. "What do you think, Raine? Can I rely on the information?"

"I only carry the packets. I have no knowledge of what is in them."

Clinton let out a laugh that made the hairs on the back of her neck stand up. Even Tully shifted uneasily from one foot to the other.

"Raine, you're delightful. I'm really glad that you decided to help Interpol try to trap me. There's a lot of your father in you, you know. By the way, where is he?"

"I don't know."

His arm shot out to close around her arm, haul her off the sofa, and bring her hard against him. "I'll find him. I've got men looking for him, even now. In the end, he'll beg me to forgive him for stealing my pearls, but I won't."

She choked back a cry. "You have the pearls back. Leave him alone."

"Not a chance. Those who cross me have to pay the price. Isn't that right, Tully?"

Tully strolled to the window, pulled the curtain aside, and peered out. "That's right."

Clinton's lips hardened with a cruel smile. "I'm going to enjoy punishing *you* most of all, Raine. Tully, come here." Clinton held out the pearls to him.

Puzzlement scored the redheaded man's rough face as he crossed the room to his boss. "What?"

"I want you to safeguard my pearls while I take Raine into the other room. And just remember, if anything should happen to that necklace, you will be the next person I punish." His words carried the deadly intent of well-aimed bullets.

All expression vanished from Tully's face. "How long will you be?"

"It depends on how cooperative Raine is," Clinton said, devouring her with a hungry look. "I might be persuaded to prolong the inevitable if she plays along." He drew a hard finger down her jawline. "What do you think, Raine? We could make this whole process quite enjoyable."

She jerked her head away from his touch. "You're despicable."

He laughed. "But didn't you know? Despicable men make the best lovers."

His fingers dug painfully into her arms through the silk of her wrapper. She had no choice but to go with him into the other room, which turned out to be a bedroom. As soon as he threw her on the bed, though, she rolled off and grabbed a table lamp. She gave a fierce tug on the cord, tearing it free of the wall outlet. Brandishing the lamp at him, she shouted, "Stay away from me."

As if he had all day, Clinton slowly removed his tie and looped it around his right hand. "What do you think you're going to do? Hit me over the head and escape? And if you did manage to get past me, do you think you could get past Tully? No, Raine. You can't escape me. I can do whatever I want with you for as long as I want. So relax. Make this something for me to remember."

With a move so quick she didn't see it coming, he knocked the lamp from her hand, grabbed her, threw her back onto the bed, and came down on top of her. The air went out of Raine's chest, and she lay there, gasping for breath.

It was the feel of his mouth on her neck that gave her new strength. She began fighting like a wild thing, kicking and clawing, but he subdued her with barely an effort.

"This won't last long at all if you keep that up," he said, wrapping his tie around her neck and drawing the ends tight. "You excite me, Raine, and have from the first moment I saw you. If only you hadn't decided to be my enemy, we could have made a great couple. Together we could have brought London to its knees." His hands were inside her wrapper, roaming over her with a hurting pressure.

She heard a scream and realized it was hers.

Then there was another loud sound, like wood splintering.

Clinton raised up and off her.

Blinking with confusion, she saw Michael bring the edge of his hand down on the back of Clinton's neck with a hard chop. Clinton crumpled to the floor, and Michael knelt and quickly handcuffed him behind his back.

Raine couldn't move. Tears streamed down her face. Even when Michael eased onto the bed beside her and pulled the wrapper back into place, she still couldn't move.

He took her into his arms. "It's over. He's not going to hurt you or anyone else."

She heard his words, but a strange kind of paralysis seemed to hold her in its grip, and she couldn't respond.

Two men bolted through the broken door. "Get

him out of here," Michael said, jerking his head to indicate Clinton, who was still out cold.

"Be glad to," one of the men said firmly.

The two men picked Clinton up and started for the door.

"Did you find anything?" Michael called after them.

The man who carried Clinton's feet answered. "The packet of bogus information was on a table, but there's no sign of that redheaded man, the Rolls, or the pearls."

"Okay, when you get Ayers secured, search around outside and see if you can find anything, but first tell Charlie I want him to drive me back to London. Right now."

Pressing a kiss to Raine's forehead, he murmured, "I'm taking you home."

He bathed her, wrapped her in a warm terry-cloth robe, took her to bed, and held her. After a long, long time, he heard her softly say, "I thought I was going to die."

"Raine, I'm so damned sorry you had to go through that." He pressed his mouth against her hair. "It was all my fault. Back at my hotel, I got this awful feeling that I had forgotten something, and then I remembered that during your phone conversation this morning with Ayers, you told him that the packet was going to be delivered to your flat. That was when I realized that I had forgotten to coordinate with Cameron the time that the packet of information would be delivered to you."

He made a sound of disgust. "Just a minor detail, right? But I had to ask myself, what if Ayers wasn't at either the club or his flat, where we expected him to be? What if he were watching your flat? After all, he could have placed that phone call from anywhere. And what if the packet were delivered before I got back? If Ayers *was* keeping an eye on your flat and had seen me leave, he also would have seen the information being delivered and would have known that he didn't have to wait. I was a damned imbecile to have left you here unprotected."

"Don't be angry with yourself. You had a lot on your mind. And you did realize what had happened, and you came to save me."

"Not soon enough," he said grimly, remembering the heart-stopping moment when he had seen her shoved into the Rolls. "And then once we turned onto the M one, we had to follow so damned far behind . . . I thought I would lose my mind."

"So did I." She turned her face into his shirt and drew in his masculine scent. It was a scent that had the power to both reassure her and to excite her.

He hugged her close. "Nothing's ever going to hurt you again. *Ever.*"

For the first time in hours, warmth began to seep into her blood. She shifted her head and gazed up at him. "Does that mean you're appointing yourself as my protector?"

"That's what it means."

Afraid to voice her question and break the peace between them, she remained silent.

But he read her mind. "I've been thinking for a long time about opening my own security business. I have the credentials. I have the contacts. It would be an *international* security business. I'm very good at what I do, and I have some ideas. I think it would be an exciting challenge."

She raised away from him in surprise. "You mean you'd resign from Interpol?"

"I have to." He brushed a strand of hair from her forehead. "I couldn't stay with them without telling them about your father."

She sat up. "You're not going to turn him in?"

"No."

"Are you sure?" she asked, concerned for him. "I mean, are you doing this just because you want to stay with me? Because if that's the reason, and deep down you really don't feel good about your decision, I'm afraid that years down the road you could very well come to resent me and hate yourself for giving up your principles."

"I won't kid you, Raine. Being with you for the rest of my life is a big part of it. I can't even conceive of living without you. But I met your father, and I liked him. As odd as it sounds, he seems such an innocent, and I'd hate to see him go to prison."

When she started to smile, he held up a hand. "Wait a minute. You should know that tomorrow he and I are going to have a serious talk, and he's going to have to see that all stolen articles that he still has are returned and promise me to give up the life of a cat burglar. Interpol won't stop looking for him, but they have no leads, and as the years go by, the file will grow dusty and be pushed farther and farther back in the bins. I think it will be all right, but he has to promise that the Ghost will retire and never be heard of again, and I have to be able to believe him, or I'll reverse my decision."

"Don't worry," she couldn't help but say. "If he's even tempted to break his promise, you won't have to turn him in, because I will murder him. But I don't think there's any real cause for concern. This episode with Clinton frightened him badly, and having you guess who he was destroyed some of his confidence."

"Your father? Somehow I doubt if his loss of confidence will last long. But, at any rate, you should know something else. I'm going to offer him a job in my new company. It will give him an income so that he won't be tempted to return to his life of crime."

"A job? Doing what, for goodness' sake?"

He smiled. "Who better to advise about security than someone who has been entering the most secure homes in Europe for the last few years."

"He'll be wonderful at it. But won't your old colleagues be suspicious?"

"They won't know the details of his job, and it will seem completely natural to have him working for me since I'm hoping that your father will soon be my father-in-law."

Joy blossomed within her, but she was afraid to let herself believe what she was hearing. Was it possible that things were going to work out? "I've got to ask you one more time, Michael. Are you very, very sure about this decision?"

"I've never been more sure of anything in my life."

"Then will you make love to me?"

His smile slowly vanished. "Raine, after what you've just been through—"

"I want you to make love to me *because* of what I've just been through. In your arms I'll forget the ugliness of the past and see the brightness of our future together."

He pulled her down beside him.

It was much later when he asked, "Do you realize that if you hadn't worn those pearls the night we met, I would still be trying to find a way to bring Ayers down?"

"Yes, and he would still be blackmailing both my father and Edward and heaven knows who else." She threaded her fingers through the hair that grew on his chest. "The thing I don't understand is why Clinton was so obsessed with the pearls. It's true they were extraordinarily beautiful, but when all was said and done, they were just a string of pearls." She paused for a moment to think. "Of course, I still don't know why I decided to wear the necklace that night. I hardly ever wear jewelry."

He idly played his fingers over the soft skin of her shoulder. "I was told that there's a legend attached to the pearls. It is said that they cannot be possessed, and that they change the life of all who come in contact with them. Whether the change is for the good or for the bad depends on whether the person is good or bad. Ayers's life was changed for the worse because of his obsession for the necklace. My life and yours were changed for the better."

"My goodness. I'm glad I didn't know all of that when I was wearing the necklace. Now I'm curious. What do you think will happen to it?"

"I don't know. I assume that Tully still has the pearls. Fencing such a fabulous necklace is going to be quite a feat, though."

With a sigh of happiness she snuggled against him. "Well, I'm just glad it's all over."

He tilted his head and smiled tenderly at her. "But it's not all over. The necklace is gone from our life, but we have each other, and our life together is just beginning."

"And it's going to be a wonderful life," she whispered, and wound her arm around his neck.

He had lived all of his eleven years in this part of New York City, Bobby thought, and he was an expert on who and what belonged in his neighborhood. The redheaded man walking on the opposite side of the street with a newspaper folded under his arm didn't belong. For one thing, no one in this neighborhood had that color hair. For another, the man was wearing a suit and tie. And he looked nervous. Bobby had learned early that if you looked like you knew what you were doing and where you were going, guys didn't bother you so much.

Bobby gave a shrug. It wasn't his problem. Besides, it was growing dark. He should go home. His mom would be worried. He hoped she had had an easy time of it today and hadn't been in too much pain. It had to be awful for her, staying in that bed day in and day out. He had never seen her cry once, but he bet she did when he was in school and his sister, Lisa, was at work. He wouldn't blame her if she did cry, but he had never even heard her complain, not even when Lisa's salary was all gone before the end of the month and they didn't have the money to buy her the medicine she needed. He felt real bad for her. One of these days, he vowed, he was going to do something really wonderful for her. One of these days . . .

He was almost at the mouth of the alley that he used as a shortcut to his apartment building when he heard a cry of surprise. He looked across the street just in time to see a guy jump out of the shadows and plunge a knife into the redheaded man's back. Bobby ducked down behind a garbage can and peered around its side.

The redheaded man was lying facedown on the sidewalk. After a quick glance up and down the street, the guy yanked the man's wallet from his back pocket, skimmed off the gold watch from his wrist, then took off running. The redheaded man didn't move. The street was strangely quiet.

Bobby hesitated. His mom had always told him

to mind his own business. But his mom had also said that people should try to help when and where they could. That man sure looked like he needed help.

Bobby darted across the street and knelt down beside him. "Mister?" He shook his shoulders. "Mister?" He picked up his wrist. It was limp and heavy. He put his face down beside the man's, but he couldn't feel any breath. Nobody could help this man now, Bobby decided, and started to get up. Then he noticed the newspaper the man had been carrying under his arm.

The newspaper was lying off to one side, partly open, and Bobby could just see the edge of a pearl. He folded the newspaper back and saw a whole string of pearls.

Gosh, he had never seen anything so pretty!

He sat back on his heels and stared at the necklace. His mom had always told him that stealing was wrong. But was it stealing if the man was dead? He didn't think so. And this necklace might cheer up his mom. It might even make her laugh. He hadn't heard her laugh in so long.

Carefully, he refolded the newspaper, hugged it to his chest, and ran toward his apartment building.

The magic of the fabulous Pearls of Sharah touches the lives of two more lovers in Fayrene Preston's next book
The Pearls of Sharah III,
LEAH'S STORY
June 1989
(on sale in May 1989)

THE EDITOR'S CORNER

Next month we celebrate our sixth year of publishing LOVESWEPT. Behind the scenes, the original team still works on the line with undiminished enthusiasm and pride. Susann is a full editor now, Nita is still the "fastest reader in the East or West," Barbara has written every single piece of back-cover copy (except the three I wrote in the first month, only proving Barbara should do them all), and from afar Elizabeth still edits one or two books each month. And I believe I can safely say that our authors' creative contributions and continuing loyalty to the line is unparalleled. From book #1 (**HEAVEN'S PRICE** by Sandra Brown) to book #329 (next month's **WAITING FOR LILA** by Billie Green) and on into the future, our authors consistently give us their best work and earn our respect and affection more each day.

Now, onward and upward for at least six more great years, here are some wonderful LOVESWEPT birthday presents for you. Joan Elliott Pickart leads off with **TO FIRST BE FRIENDS,** LOVESWEPT #324. Shep Templeton was alive! The award-winning journalist, the only man Emily Templeton had ever loved, hadn't died in the Pataguam jungle, but was coming home—only to learn his wife had divorced him. Eight months before, after a night of reckless passion, he had left for his dangerous assignment. She'd vowed then it was the last time Shep would leave her. Love for Emily was all that had kept Shep going, had made him want to live through months of pain and recovery. Now he had to fight for a new start. . . . Remember, this marvelous book is also available in a beautiful hardcover collector's edition from Doubleday.

In **BOUND TO HAPPEN,** LOVESWEPT #325, by Mary Kay McComas, a breathtaking angel drives Joe Bonner off the road, calls him a trespasser, then faints dead away in his arms. Leslie Rothe had run away from her sister's wedding in confusion, wondering if she'd ever fall

(continued)

in love—or if she even wanted to. Joe awakened turbulent emotions, teased her unmercifully, then kissed her breathless, and taught a worldly woman with an innocent heart how it felt to love a man. But could she prove how much she treasured Joe before her folly destroyed their love?

Next, we introduce an incredibly wonderful treat to you. Deborah Smith begins her Cherokee Trilogy with **SUNDANCE AND THE PRINCESS,** LOVESWEPT #325. (The second romance in the trilogy, **TEMPTING THE WOLF,** will be on sale in June; the final love story, **KAT'S TALE,** will be on sale in August.) In **SUNDANCE AND THE PRINCESS** Jeopard Surprise is Robert Redford gorgeous, a golden-haired outlaw whose enigmatic elegance enthralls Tess Gallatin, makes her want to break all the rules—and lose herself in his arms! He'd come aboard her boat pretending to court the blue-eyed Cherokee princess, but his true mission—to search for a stolen diamond—was endangered by Tess's sweet, seductive laugh. Tess could deny Jep nothing, not her deepest secrets or her mother's precious remembrance, but she never suspected her lover might betray her . . . or imagined how fierce his fury might blaze. An incandescent love story, not to be missed.

LOST IN THE WILD, LOVESWEPT #327, by Gail Douglas, features impossibly gorgeous Nick Corcoran, whose mesmerizing eyes make Tracy Carlisle shiver with desire. But her shyness around her grandfather's corporate heir apparent infuriates her! For three years Nick had considered her off limits, and besides, he had no intention of romancing the snobbish granddaughter of his powerful boss to win the top job. But when Tracy outsmarted a pair of kidnappers and led him into the forest in a desperate escape plan, Nick was enchanted by this courageous woodswoman who embraced danger and risked her life to save his. But could Tracy persuade Nick that by choice she wasn't his rival, only his prize?

(continued)

Peggy Webb gives us pure dynamite in **ANY THURS-DAY,** LOVESWEPT #328. Hannah Donovan is a sexy wildcat of a woman, Jim Roman decided as she pointed her rifle at his chest—definitely a quarry worthy of his hunt! With a devilish, devastating smile, the rugged columnist began his conquest of this beautiful Annie Oakley by kissing her with expert, knowing lips . . . and Hannah felt wicked, wanton passion brand her cool scientist's heart. Jim wore power and danger like a cloak, challenged and intrigued her as few men ever had—but she had to show him she couldn't be tamed . . . or possessed. Could they stop fighting destiny and each other long enough to bridge their separate worlds? A fabulous romance!

Remember Dr. Delilah Jones? In **WAITING FOR LILA,** LOVESWEPT #329, Billie Green returns to her characters of old for a raucous good time. Lila had special plans for the medical conference in Acapulco—this trip she was determined to bag a husband! She enlisted her best friends as matchmakers, invited them to produce the perfect candidate—rich, handsome, successful—then spotted the irresistibly virile man of her dreams all by herself. Bill Shelley was moonstruck by the elegant lady with the voice like raw silk, captivated by this mysterious, seductive angel who seemed to have been made just for him. Once he knew her secrets, could Bill convince her that nothing would keep her as safe and happy as his enduring love? A pure delight from Billie!

Enjoy!

Carolyn Nichols

Carolyn Nichols
Editor
LOVESWEPT
Bantam Books
666 Fifth Avenue
New York, NY 10103